FORBIDDEN PASSIONS

Visit us at www.boldstrokesbooks.com

By the Author

Forbidden Passions

Shots Fired

FORBIDDEN PASSIONS

by

MJ Williamz

2011

FORBIDDEN PASSIONS

© 2011 By MJ Williamz. All Rights Reserved.

ISBN 10: 1-60282-641-2
ISBN 13: 978-1-60282-641-0

This Trade Paperback Original Is Published By
Bold Strokes Books, Inc.
P.O. Box 249
Valley Falls, NY 12185

First Edition: September 2011

Credits
Editor: Cindy Cresap
Production Design: Susan Ramundo
Cover Design By Sheri (graphicartist2020@hotmail.com)

Acknowledgments

First and foremost, I'd like to thank my son for always believing in me. Next, my sincere gratitude to ABR for making the time to keep up with me to get this book written and beta'd in record time. For my friends on Facebook, thank you for reading the blurbs and encouraging me on my path. A special thanks to Nat for just being Nat and supporting me in all my endeavors.

Last, but not least, huge thank-yous to Cindy Cresap for her patient editing and Rad for giving authors a home where we can be true to ourselves.

Dedication

To my Facebook friends who were with me
every step of the way.

CHAPTER ONE

The sun was setting over Belle Vierge, the grand plantation that belonged to the widow Della Prentiss. Bright oranges and pinks filled the sky as the carriage pulled to a stop in front of the main house. Corrine Staples stepped out without waiting for the driver to open the door. She saw his look of disgust at her attire of trousers and jacket, but ignored it. She was used to it. As a woman working in a man's field of accounting, she met with disparaging looks and comments from men all the time. Only those that truly knew her accepted her, and then just barely.

She allowed him to get her trunk, however, as she hurried up the front steps and into the waiting arms of her childhood best friend, Della Prentiss. It had been five years since they'd seen each other. Five long years that had included a yellow fever outbreak that had cost Della her husband and left her to raise her spitfire daughter alone.

"It's so good to see you, Della," Corrine whispered into Della's red hair. She stepped back. "I'm just sorry for the circumstances that have brought me here. You've lost weight. Are you well?"

"I'm fine," Della said. "Thank you for coming. Who would have imagined the last time we saw each other what horrible things would happen before we got together again? And now there's money missing from the plantation. I do hope you can get to the bottom of it."

"I will do my very best. I was so sorry to hear about Theodore. How long has it been now?"

"Thank you, it's been almost two years."

"Tell me, how's little Katie?"

"She's not so little, and she's more than a handful." Della paused to stare at her. "And how are you, Cori? How's business? I must say, you must hear so much working in a man's world. I can't imagine what that would be like. What are people saying about this Lincoln fellow being elected? Are you hearing talk of secession? I declare, where are my manners? Won't you please come in?"

Corrine held the door and followed Della into her front room. The black curtains were drawn, and the large mirror at the foot of the staircase was covered. Corrine felt a deep sympathy for Della to be widowed at the age of thirty-seven.

Della motioned to a chair, and Corrine sat but declined the tea Della offered.

"Do you have any brandy in the house?" she asked.

Della looked shocked for a moment but quickly regained her composure. She rang a bell, and Theodore's manservant appeared. "Pierre, will you please get some brandy for Miss Staples?"

Pierre bowed and left the room. When he was out of earshot, Della said, "I haven't had the heart to let him go yet."

"It does no harm to keep him on."

Pierre reappeared with a glass of brandy. He set it in front of Corrine then silently exited again.

Della watched as Corrine took a sip of the warm amber liquid. "Don't tell me you'll be wanting a cigar as well."

"Never before dinner." Corrine smiled. "Don't be so shocked. It's the life I lead. I'd have one after dinner with Theodore if he were here."

She realized the harm of her thoughtless words as she saw Della's eyes glisten with tears.

"I am so sorry, Della." She was immediately across the room and holding her. "How insensitive of me to say such a thing."

"I just can't believe he's not coming home."

"I can't believe it either."

They both jumped when a young woman with rich auburn hair burst into the room.

"Why is Mama crying? What did you do to her?"

"Now, now, Kathleen, where are your manners? You say hello to Miss Staples properly."

Kathleen stood still, emerald eyes hard as stone as she stared at Corrine.

"I said something that made your mother cry." Corrine stood and took in the beautiful young woman her little Katie had grown into. "I have apologized to her, and now I apologize to you."

Kathleen crossed the room, sat next to her mother, and hugged her. "Mama, are you okay?"

"I'm fine. Now stop being so rude to our guest."

Kathleen remained seated and looked back at Corrine. Her eyes had softened somewhat, and Corrine was surprised at the fluttering in her crotch. This was little Katie Prentiss she was looking at.

"I must say, Katie, you've certainly grown into quite the young woman."

Katie stood and curtsied. "Thank you, Miss Staples. It's so very nice to see you again."

She stood tall again and eyed Corrine with an air of mischief. Corrine was grateful Katie couldn't know what she was thinking as she took in her décolletage. The swell of her young breasts did little to quell the burning that had begun in Corrine's loins.

"I'm trying to remember," she said. "How old were you when I last saw you? Do you recall my last visit? We went for a long horseback ride all over the plantation."

"I remember that." Katie favored Corrine with a radiant smile of perfect white teeth. "I believe I was fourteen at the time."

Which would make her of legal age, Corrine thought.

"It's time to get ready for dinner. Why don't we all change and meet back down here in half an hour?"

Della's voice startled Corrine back to reality. She had honestly forgotten Della was there.

"Katie, will you please show Miss Staples to her room?"

Corrine followed the swishing skirts of Katie up the sweeping staircase and down the expansive hallway until they reached her door.

"Thank you, Katie. I appreciate your hospitality."

"My pleasure, Miss Staples. I'll see you downstairs."

❖

Exactly thirty minutes later, Della and Corrine were sitting at the dining room table.

"I do apologize for Kathleen's behavior. I can't believe she's late. I declare I raised her with better manners."

"Not to worry, Della. She's still young. I think we were all a bit irresponsible at her age."

"Not me. I had a year-old baby when I was her age."

Corrine laughed. "So you did. And what a lovely woman your baby has grown into." She stood as Katie entered the dining room.

"Nice of you to join us," Della said as Katie took her seat across from Corrine.

"I'm sorry I'm late. I lost track of time."

Corrine studied Katie's face and appreciatively noted her lips were painted, and there was color added to her cheeks.

Her mother noticed as well. "Kathleen Prentiss! What are you wearing?"

"I just wanted to feel dressed up."

"This is my dining room, not a brothel. I'll thank you not to wear so much paint in the future."

Corrine studied the napkin in her lap until she was certain she could keep the smile from her face.

"What's it like working with men, Miss Staples? Do they take you seriously?" Katie asked

Something in Katie's tone made Corrine take note. The question was innocent enough, but the way it was asked suggested more of a challenge.

"Why, yes, they do. I've been keeping books on the docks for ten years now. I took over the business when my father passed. I've earned the respect of the men."

"Do you really feel you have to dress like a man to get their respect?"

Corrine was amused. "I gain their respect by being smart and honest. I've also found that dressing as I do helps keep them focused on the work at hand. I can't imagine trying to focus on work with you if you were dressed as you are now. I'd find that rather distracting."

She saw more color rise to Katie's cheeks, but the conversation stopped as Maddy served them the main course.

"This is delicious, Della. The chicken is so tender." Corrine hoped to keep the subject from ending up back in Katie's control. She felt as though Katie was trying to get a rise out of her.

"Where do you even find trousers that fit you?" Katie asked.

"I go to a tailor."

"A tailor? But when he measures you, doesn't he have to touch your—"

"Kathleen!" Della said. "That is quite enough. Honestly. Miss Staples is our guest. Please try to remember that."

Corrine fought the urge to come to Katie's defense. She had found Katie's attempts at irreverence rather amusing, but didn't want to undermine Della's authority, tenuous as it was.

The rest of the meal passed without incident, and after dessert, Corrine stood and excused herself.

"I am tired from my journey and have some work to review, so I would like to retire now. Thank you again for a delicious dinner and"—she turned to Katie—"the spirited conversation."

❖

Alone in her room, Corrine removed her waistcoat and shirt and hung them before sitting to go over the books she had brought with her. She was lost in the calculations when she heard a knock on the door.

Assuming it was one of the staff, she absently called, "Come in."

"Miss Staples?"

Corrine turned at Katie's rich voice. She stood when she saw the vision of Katie in a white cotton nightgown that clung to her full breasts, the outlines of which were visible under the thin fabric.

She forced her gaze up to Katie's eyes and realized then how exposed she was in her undershirt and trousers. She felt her nipples harden as Katie finally drew her focus away from Corrine's small breasts.

Corrine slid her hands in her pockets in an attempt to look less uncomfortable.

"Katie. What brings you here?"

"I wanted to apologize for my behavior at dinner."

"Oh, really, that's not necessary." Corrine smiled. "I appreciate it, and I'm sure your mother put you up to this, but really, I was not offended."

Katie flushed and continued indignantly. "Mother had nothing to do with this. I felt as if we'd gotten off on the wrong foot, and I came to say I'm sorry of my own accord."

"Well then, thank you. I appreciate that." Corrine tried not to sound condescending. "I do hope our time together will be more pleasant from here on out."

Katie curtsied slightly, causing her breasts to jiggle, and then said good night.

When the door was closed, Corrine sank in her chair, her whole body on fire. She hadn't planned on needing a trip into town this soon, but she decided she'd better go the next day or risk doing something foolish.

❖

Katie lay on her bed, trying to stop the visions of Miss Staples from running through her head. It was no use. She pictured her mother wrapped in Miss Staples's arms when she first came home that evening. She envisioned her looking so dapper in the men's clothes she brazenly wore. Katie had never seen such a thing and found herself titillated at the sight. She saw Miss Staples's long, strong fingers as she ate her dinner. She saw the twinkle in her eye and half smile as she answered Katie's questions. And finally, she saw her as she was in her room just then, her muscular arms bare and her firm breasts barely concealed by her undershirt.

Miss Corrine Staples was a very handsome woman. And something told Katie she was no stranger to giving pleasure to another woman. She got out of bed and locked her bedroom door, then slid her sleeves down her arms and stepped out of her nightgown.

She stood in front of the full-length mirror and tried to see herself as Miss Staples might. She held her heavy breasts up for inspection and noted her erect nipples were dusky pink and in sharp contrast to her pale skin. She ran her hands down her flat belly to where her legs met, imagining briefly Miss Staples's fingers on her slick clit.

Giving in to her newest guilty pleasure, Katie pulled a chair in front of the mirror and sat. She watched herself as she fondled her breasts, pressing them together and kneading them as her pulse began to quicken. She felt the wetness between her legs as she watched herself tug and twist her nipples, sending waves of pleasure throughout her body.

She played with her breasts until she could no longer stand it. She sank low in the chair and spread her legs, treating herself to a perfect view of her swollen lips and throbbing clit. She watched as her cunt swallowed three of her fingers, then she closed her eyes and envisioned Miss Staples's thin lips on her as she rubbed her needy clit.

The need to see was not as great as the need to fantasize, and she gave herself over to thoughts of Miss Staples having her way with her. She imagined her biting her nipples while her hand fucked her. She spread her legs wider to take her deeper. Suddenly, Miss Staples was everywhere—on her and in her.

She imagined it was Miss Staples's tongue hard at work on her clit, and she rubbed it fast and furiously until the orgasm finally shot through her body. She bit her lip to keep from crying out Miss Staples's name.

Not satisfied, she repeated the fantasies and the actions again and again until finally she was exhausted and thoroughly spent. She put her nightgown back on and climbed into bed where she fell into a fitful sleep.

CHAPTER TWO

Corrine and Della were having coffee the next morning when Katie came downstairs in her pale green wrapper. Corrine smiled and said good morning and swore she saw Katie blush.

"How are you this morning?" Corrine asked.

"I'm fine." She took in the silk trousers and jacket Corrine wore. "Why are you dressed so early?"

"I have to go into town today to tend to some business."

"I can't believe your business won't keep," Della said, coughing into her handkerchief. "Your visit's only just begun."

"I am sorry about that, Della, but I discovered something while looking over the books last night. I'm afraid it can't wait." She added, "Are you sure you're healthy?"

"I'm fine. Please don't worry about me."

"I want to go to town." Katie radiated excitement. "May I please go along? Please?"

Corrine's stomach clenched. The idea of spending a day with Katie appealed to her in ways that made it most unappealing.

"I would love to take you, Katie, but it's business, and I'm afraid you'd be bored to tears."

"But what if I enjoy business?" Katie said.

"Kathleen Prentiss!" Della said. "A lady has no place in business."

"But Miss Staples enjoys it. Maybe I would too."

"I'm not the type of woman your mother would like you to grow up to become. She has plans for you to meet some nice man and marry him, not work alongside one."

"What if I keep myself occupied while you see to your business?"

"Kathleen," Della interjected. "How dare you suggest gallivanting about New Orleans without accompaniment? I'll not hear of such a thing."

"You're being so unfair. I'm a grown woman now. I just want to have some fun and you never let me."

"What if I promise to take you to New Orleans another time?" Corrine heard herself say.

"Fine. But what am I supposed to do today? I declare, you two are conspiring to make my life miserable." She stormed out of the room.

"I'm afraid I must apologize again for her behavior. I don't know what's gotten into her."

"She seems to have a lot of anger inside. Maybe I'm an easy target because, after a five-year absence, I'm almost a stranger to her."

"That's still no excuse."

"I appreciate what you're saying, Della, but I'm willing to give the girl some leeway."

"And I appreciate that, but I won't tolerate her behaving so unladylike and being rude to my guest."

Corrine took a sip of the rich chicory roast. Della's words hit home. She was a guest in Della's home and had no right to think about her daughter in such an unsavory fashion.

"Now then, if you'll excuse me, I need to take my leave. Which horse did you say I could borrow?"

"The roan is the one Theodore used to take to town. He's steady and sure and won't shy around the traffic and crowds."

Corrine took her books and cut through the kitchen and across the expansive lawn to get to the stables. She was loading the saddlebags when Katie showed up dressed in a dark green riding habit.

"I still wish you'd take me with you," she said.

Corrine involuntarily looked her up and down. The bodice accentuated her full breasts, while the skirt showed off her trim hips.

"You heard your mother." It came out harsher than she'd meant it.

"I did, but if you told her you wanted to take me, I'm sure she'd allow it."

If she knew *how* I wanted to take you, she'd kick me out of her house, Corrine mused.

"I'm a guest in your mother's house, Katie. I must abide by her wishes as surely as you."

"What if I just happen to follow you?" Katie said, lovingly stroking the neck of the roan.

She was less than a foot away from Corrine, and Corrine was having a hard time concentrating.

"If you were to do that, I'd simply turn around and come back. And then neither of us would be successful, would we?"

Katie locked her hands behind her hips and stepped closer to Corrine. "You don't like me much, do you?"

Corrine stumbled as she hurriedly stepped back from the approaching breasts. "Now that's not fair, Katie. You know you've always been special to me."

"That was when I was a child. I don't think you like the woman I've become."

"We haven't had a lot of time together since I've arrived, but I find you to be an interesting woman."

"If you took me to town with you, we'd be spending time together, and you might find that I'm more than simply interesting."

"I promise you I will take you to town. Just not today. Please understand that I simply must not allow you to accompany me."

"Fine, I'll go for a ride by myself." She walked away, leaving Corrine fairly salivating at the sight of her tight ass.

Corrine mounted the roan and urged him on to a quick pace as she escaped the hotbed of the stables. Shaking all over, she needed to get as far away from Katie as possible. Katie had no idea what she was doing to her, and Corrine wanted nothing more than to show her how she had begun to feel about her.

But that would be wrong, she thought as she tried to get her mind off Katie. The rubbing of her swollen clit against her trousers as she rode did little to assuage the need that was almost at a boiling point.

Thirty minutes later, Corrine pulled her horse up in front of a vast Spanish-style house. It was painted a light yellow and had dark green trim. The curtains were drawn on the main window, but the sound of piano tunes and laughter floated on the air. She glanced up and saw several attractive young women on the widow's walk above.

She tied the roan and climbed the steps. She took a moment to straighten her jacket and slacks, then wiped her face with a handkerchief. It was already warm, and she had worked up a sweat on the ride in.

Deciding she was ready, she knocked on the door in a pattern she had learned years ago. A girl younger even than Katie answered the door.

"Is Miss Cantrall in?" Corrine asked.

The young girl opened the door and let Corrine in. "May I tell her who's calling?"

"It's Corrine Staples."

The girl showed Corrine to an anteroom that was blocked off from the rest of the house. The French doors that led to the living room also had curtains drawn, but Corrine couldn't help but hear the raucous group on the other side.

"If you'll have a seat"—the girl motioned to a loveseat—"I'll tell Miss Cantrall you're here."

Corrine had barely sat down when in bustled a plump older blonde wearing a long pink dress. Her face bore more makeup than Corrine remembered, but she reminded herself it had been five years since she'd been there. Miss Cantrall approached her with her arms open wide.

"Corrine! My Lord, aren't you a sight for sore eyes?" She held her to her ample bosom that threatened to break loose from its confining bodice. "How have you been?"

"I've been good, Miss Cantrall. I see the years have treated you kindly."

"Oh, you are too sweet. But I must say you are cutting as handsome a figure as ever. Did Shirley offer you a drink?"

"She did not, but not to worry. I didn't come here to drink."

"I'd imagine not. I'm sorry to tell you that Margaret moved on a couple of years ago, but we have some new girls, and I'm sure you'll find them to your liking."

"And they'll be fine that I'm a woman?"

"I wouldn't suggest them otherwise, my dear. Now let me think who's here today. We have a lovely redhead named Catherine that I highly recommend."

Corrine smiled at the irony. "She sounds perfect."

"Upstairs or downstairs or does it matter?"

"Downstairs, please, as I am sorely in need of a bath."

Miss Cantrall threw open the French doors and stood perusing the room until her gaze fell on a voluptuous redhead who appeared to be in her mid-twenties. She beckoned her with a crooked finger.

The woman stood at the entrance of the anteroom, both examining and being examined by Corrine. She had light red hair that hung to the middle of her back and had been brushed until it shone. Her large breasts were barely contained in the bodice of her green satin dress. Corrine thought if Catherine moved slightly in the wrong manner, her nipples would surely be exposed. Her face was colored lightly, just enough to accentuate her beauty, rather than having to hide her age.

Corrine stood and extended a hand. "So nice to meet you, Kathleen."

"It's Catherine," the woman corrected her kindly as she placed her hand in Corrine's.

"I apologize. I shall not make that mistake again." Corrine bent and kissed Catherine's knuckles.

"Aren't you the gentlewoman?" Catherine said.

Corrine smiled.

"I'll leave you two alone now," Miss Cantrall said. "Room four is open and will have a hot bath if you two don't mind visiting for a bit."

Corrine motioned to the loveseat. "Please."

"After you," Catherine said.

Corrine sat and Catherine sat in her lap and placed her arm around Corrine's shoulders.

Corrine snaked her arm around Catherine's waist and pulled her tight. She was enjoying the soft breasts so close to her face.

"Is this your first trip to Miss Cantrall's?" Catherine asked.

"Oh, no. I've been coming here for years."

"Strange that we haven't met."

"I live in Baton Rouge. I haven't been to New Orleans in five years."

"That would explain it. What brings you to our fine city today?"

"I'm staying with friends nearby. I had the need of your services, though, so here I am."

"Well, I hope you'll find everything to your satisfaction."

"I have no doubt everything will be just fine." She smiled and traced her finger along the tops of Catherine's breasts.

Shirley appeared in the doorway. "Your bath is ready."

Catherine stood and Corrine followed her down the hallway to a bedroom with a four-poster bed and a large claw-foot tub set off to the side. There were two straight back chairs, both red to match the red quilt on the bed and the deep red curtains.

Catherine began unbuttoning Corrine's shirt. Corrine stood still, watching Catherine's deft fingers work. Once her shirt and undershirt were removed, Catherine dropped to her knees and unbuttoned Corrine's trousers. Corrine stepped out of them, and Catherine placed her cheek on Corrine's inner thigh.

"It's always such a treat to have a woman customer." She gazed at Corrine's core between her legs. She moved closer, but Corrine stopped her.

"I am very much in need of a bath."

She climbed into the oversized tub and sank to her chin in bubbles.

"May I help you bathe?" Catherine asked.

"In due time. For now, I'd like you to undress for me. Slowly."

Catherine untied the bodice of her gown and slid it down her arms, leaving her breasts bare.

Corrine felt a stirring deep within as she looked at the large, pale mounds with the hard pink nipples.

"Very nice," she said. "Show me how you like to have them played with."

Catherine never took her gaze from Corrine's eyes as she pinched the base of her nipples, then slid her fingers to their tips and twisted. Corrine's focus never left the tits.

"I'd like you to continue undressing now."

Catherine stepped out of the dress and her hoops until she stood in only her bloomers.

"Are you aroused yet?" Corrine asked.

Catherine swallowed and nodded.

"Take those off and hand them to me."

Catherine did as instructed. Corrine held the damp crotch of the bloomers to her nose. "You are quite aroused. And you smell divine."

Corrine tossed the bloomers to one side and stared at the naked goddess on display. Her own cunt was wet, and she couldn't wait to take the luscious Catherine. She continued to allow her gaze to roam all over Catherine until she began to squirm.

"What's wrong?" Corrine asked. "Is it not all right for me to admire the body I am paying for?"

"Your stare is so intense."

"I find you quite beautiful."

"Thank you."

"Lie on the bed and spread your legs for me. I want to have a look at you."

Catherine did as she was told, and it was all Corrine could do to remain in the tub. Her heart was racing and her clit throbbing. The sight of Catherine's slick cunt was almost more than she could stand.

"Touch yourself. Dip your fingers inside."

Catherine's eyes closed halfway as she followed the instructions.

"Now come here."

Catherine stepped over to the tub and Corrine grabbed her wrist. She raised Catherine's hand to her mouth and sucked greedily on her coated fingers.

"Join me in the tub."

As Catherine stood with one foot in the tub and one on the floor, Corrine slid her hand up Catherine's leg. She ran her fingers over her clit.

Catherine stood still, her eyes closed.

"Come on. Sit down facing me."

Once Catherine was seated, Corrine slipped her fingers into Catherine's mouth. It was Catherine's turn to suck greedily.

"Oh my, you do know how to suck, don't you?"

"Comes with the job." Catherine smiled.

Corrine leaned forward and put her hand behind Catherine's neck, pulling her close. She lowered her mouth to Catherine's and kissed her hard. There was no need for the pretense of tenderness. She was there to fuck, and that's what Catherine was paid to do.

As their tongues moved over each other and Corrine's passion burned out of control, Kathleen's face appeared in Corrine's mind. She sat back abruptly.

"What's wrong?"

"Nothing." Corrine tried to lose the image in her head. "I just needed some air after that kiss."

Catherine got on her knees and leaned her breasts into Corrine's. "Let's pick up where we left off."

Corrine kissed her deeply and didn't care if visions of Kathleen returned. She'd love to be in the tub with her, and while she'd never act on it, she certainly couldn't deny it.

She ran her hands through Catherine's hair and kept her close. "I think it's time you wash me," Corrine said when they broke for air again.

Corrine turned in the tub while Catherine fished the washrag out of the water. She closed her eyes as Catherine slowly and deliberately rubbed circles on her back. She drew in her breath as Catherine dragged the cloth along her neck, allowing trickles of water to escape forward to tease her chest and drip off her sensitive nipples.

Satisfied that her back was clean, Corrine turned around and lay back for Catherine to continue her ministrations.

Catherine started at her neckline and slowly drew the rag downward. Corrine gasped when Catherine lifted her small breasts and took her time washing under them. Volcanic heat shot through her when Catherine pinched each erect nipple and twisted gently.

Corrine closed her eyes as Catherine's mouth replaced the washrag, and she sucked and tugged on first one nipple, then the other. She struggled to maintain her composure when she felt the rough rag on her turgid clit.

She pulled Catherine to her and kissed her again as she felt soapy fingers inside her hot cunt.

She broke the kiss. "I do believe I'm clean. You may get out. Dry yourself slowly for me."

Catherine grabbed a large towel and stepped out of the tub. She took her time rubbing the towel over her large breasts as Corrine looked on appreciatively.

"Place your foot here as you dry between your legs." Corrine patted the side of the tub.

Catherine did as she was instructed and rubbed her folds and clit while Corrine watched. She dropped her towel when she was dry and reached for another one. She held it open for Corrine to step into. Corrine kissed Catherine as she wrapped the towel around her and dried her back. She fondled Catherine's breasts and ran her thumbs over the nipples, loving how they reacted to her touch.

Catherine stepped back and dried Corrine's front, then slid the towel between her legs and wiped the soapy water off. She dropped to her knees and placed her face between Corrine's legs.

Corrine helped her to stand and saw the pout on her face. "I want to spend forever down there," said Catherine.

Corrine kissed her, running her tongue into Catherine's mouth and tasting her own arousal. She was light-headed when the kiss ended.

"Go lie on the bed. Keep your legs open."

Catherine lay on her back, her head on the pillows, knees bent and legs spread.

"Very nice. You have a beautiful twat."

She climbed over the foot of the bed and kissed Catherine's plump thighs. She pressed her chest against Catherine's wet folds and slid along it as she trailed kisses up her soft belly to her full breasts. She suckled one nipple and then the other while she kneaded and caressed the soft mounds.

She moved her hand lower, over the slippery clit that stood begging for attention, and into the waiting wetness. She plunged three fingers inside as deep as they would go, then pulled them out. She thrust them in again. Once more, she withdrew them.

Corrine propped herself on an elbow and watched Catherine's face as she fucked her. She smiled as Catherine's eyes flew open with each rough entry, then pleaded with hers as she withdrew her hand.

Corrine drove four fingers inside the hot cunt and twisted them around before taking them out again. Once more, she pushed into her and left them in, thrusting harder and harder with each stroke.

Corrine slid her wet hand out and moved between Catherine's legs.

"Hold your knees back."

Catherine grabbed her knees and pulled them back. Corrine slipped her whole hand inside the gaping cunt. She made a fist and inserted it deep inside Catherine.

"Oh, fuck! That feels good!"

"You like that, huh? I figured a good whore could take what I give."

She buried her arm past her wrist and twisted it again. The tight walls were pressing in on her, crushing her hand, but she knew the pressure she was giving was much stronger. She continued to gently punch Catherine's internal pleasure zone over and over until her juices were running down her arm.

"Yes!" Catherine screamed. "Please give it to me."

Corrine could no longer ignore the pink pearl that stuck out from under its hood. She rubbed it as hard as she could with her left thumb while she continued to fuck Catherine with her fist.

Catherine's head thrashed on the pillows as she continued to hold her legs back and leave herself open for Corrine. Corrine pulled her hand out and placed it in Catherine's mouth, gagging her while she continued to rub her clit.

"Do you taste good?"

Catherine nodded, her mouth still full. Her whole body began to shake as Corrine continued to rub her clit. She stilled briefly then shuddered in release.

Corrine removed her hand from Catherine's mouth and pinched her clit before lying on her back. Her whole body was on fire, her own clit throbbing after such an intense fuck.

Catherine leaned in to kiss her, but Corrine placed her hand on top of Catherine's head and forced her between her legs.

Catherine licked Corrine, starting at her wet hole and flattening her tongue as she worked toward her clit. Corrine felt the tongue circle her clit and then repeat the process.

"Don't tease me. Just fuck me."

She felt Catherine's talented tongue deep inside her while her fingers pressed into her swollen clit.

The sensations had Corrine dizzy with need. She arched her hips to take Catherine deeper and pressed against the back of her head to hold her in place. Her whole body exploded as she finally gave herself over to the release she so desperately craved.

"Will I see you again?" Catherine asked.

"I will seek your services as need arises while I'm here."

A much more relaxed Corrine mounted her horse and took a slower, more leisurely trip home.

CHAPTER THREE

Corrine, Della, and Katie sat on wooden rockers in the shade of the front porch, the day unseasonably hot for October. Nobody had much to say, the heat and humidity seeming to have sucked the conversation from them.

Corrine wiped the perspiration from her neck with her handkerchief and felt sorry for Della and Katie who looked positively miserable in the high-neck, long-sleeved black dresses they had worn to Mass. She understood the period of mourning in respect for Theodore, but she wondered who would have noticed if they were in their own homes dressed more appropriately for the heat.

They were dreading Maddy calling them into the house for lunch. The wooden fans creaked in resistance to the work they were doing and did little to add to the comfort inside.

"Someone's coming!" Katie stood and tried to see who was creating the cloud of dust coming up the drive.

"Who is it?" Della asked.

"It's Thomas." Katie lifted her skirts and ran down the steps.

"Kathleen," Della called after her. "You get up here. We do not go running after young men." She looked at Corrine, frustration etched on her face.

Katie had stopped halfway down the front steps and turned to wait for Thomas at the top.

Thomas removed his hat and climbed the stairs, his face alight at the sight of Katie.

"Miss Katie." He bowed slightly, then walked past to Della.

"Mrs. Prentiss."

"Thomas. Corrine," Della said, "this is Thomas DuPre. His family owns the Sugar Magnolia plantation. Thomas, I'd like you to meet my dearest friend, Corrine Staples."

Corrine stood and shook hands with the gentleman who clearly didn't know what to make of a woman in trousers.

"Ma'am."

"What brings you out here on a day the devil himself must surely be seeking the cool?"

"I came to call on Miss Katie."

Corrine stood only an inch or two shorter than Thomas and continued to look him in the eye. "Do you honestly find it appropriate to come calling while they are still in mourning?"

"Miss Staples! You're being rude to my guest," Katie said.

Corrine couldn't stop herself. She wanted to send this young man away and tell him to keep his grimy paws off her Katie. Jealousy was an unfamiliar emotion for her, but she wanted to make sure nothing untoward happened between Katie and Thomas.

"I did not know they are still in mourning. I will be happy to take my leave if you deem this inappropriate."

"Don't listen to her." Katie was at his side. "I'm glad you came out. Besides, I'm no longer in mourning."

Obviously uncertain what to do, Della walked over to the others. "He's had a rather long journey and must be thirsty. I wouldn't feel right turning him away just yet."

"All right, you two may sit here on the front porch and visit. I'll have Maddy bring you some sweet tea," Corrine said.

"You're not my father, and you'll not tell me what I will or will not do!" Katie shot at her. She grabbed the stunned Thomas by the hand and dragged him around to the side steps. "Come on," she said to him. "Let's go look at the horses."

"Kathleen!" Della called after her, but she ignored her. Katie kept her hand firmly on Thomas, who was obviously uncomfortable with this turn of events.

"I'll go after her," Corrine said.

"No, don't bother." Della doubled over in a coughing fit. "That poor lad is already mortified. I'll speak with Katie tonight."

❖

Katie pulled Thomas into the cool of the stables.

"Do you think that was such a good idea, Katie? Didn't you hear your mother call after us?"

"I don't know who Miss Staples thinks she is coming into our house and trying to make the rules. I'll not listen to her."

"But your mother…"

"I'll simply say I didn't hear her. Now, would you relax?"

"I sure could have used some tea, though."

"We'll fetch us some later. At least it's cool in here with the horses."

"That it is. Although the stench isn't exactly what I feel pleasant to share with a lady such as yourself."

"I love the smell of horses." She walked down the aisle, inhaling deeply. She came to the roan's stall, and her memory took her back to two days prior when she had begged Miss Staples to take her to New Orleans. Miss Staples had looked so handsome as she readied the horse. Katie still fumed that she'd told her no. She wasn't used to being denied, and she hoped she'd made that clear to Miss Staples.

Thomas looked around nervously. "I still don't know that it's right for us to be unchaperoned."

"Must you be so afraid of those old women? Talk to me about something else. Let me know how happy you are that you came to call on me."

The stables had always been a happy place for Katie. She'd had many an afternoon tryst there but certainly wouldn't share that with Thomas. But since he was visiting, she felt he could at least amuse her.

"What would you like me to talk to you about?"

Katie spun to face him. "Oh, please tell me news of the upcoming election. What do you know about this damned Lincoln? Will he win? What will that mean for us?"

"Miss Katie! Must you swear? And politics is not something a gentleman discusses with a lady."

Katie thought again of Miss Staples. She reckoned Miss Staples knew about Lincoln and secession. She wondered how shocked she'd be if Katie asked her about it. Clearly, Thomas would be no help.

"Besides, Katie, with you just losing your daddy…I mean, I just imagine it would be too much for you to even think about such things."

"I think about lots of things." She smiled coquettishly and brushed against him.

Thomas cleared his throat. "I really am parched. I do believe we should make our way back to the house."

"But I thought you wanted to know what I think about." Her mouth was inches from his face.

He stepped back. "I certainly know there are things a lady shouldn't think about and should certainly never discuss."

"What do you think about, Thomas?"

"I think about many things, Miss Katie. I think about the plantation, about what might happen if slavery were to be abolished. I think of important things such as that. Nothing that wouldn't bore a fine lady, I'm afraid."

"I find it funny that you add 'Miss' in front of my name when you're nervous."

"I use it at times when I feel you need to be reminded of propriety."

"You worry too much, Thomas DuPre."

"I fear that if I'm ever to be allowed to call again, we should get back to the house."

"Fine. Take me back to the house."

Katie decided to have some fun and tease Thomas. He was at the opening of the stables when he turned to see what was taking her so long. His eyes widened as he stared at her neckline where she had unbuttoned the top three buttons on her dress.

"Miss Katie! Whatever do you think you're doing?"

"I'm hot." She grinned.

"Do you know how that will look to them?"

"I certainly know how it looks to me," Corrine said, appearing in the doorway.

Thomas flushed and stammered, "I did not touch her, ma'am. I swear!"

Corrine seethed as she stared him down. "You may say that all you like, but it certainly looks different from where I'm standing."

"I'm sure it does, but we were just leaving, and when I turned around—"

"When you turned around, you saw the lovely vision of the young Miss Prentiss and couldn't keep your hands off her? Leave here at once."

Corrine didn't turn as he scampered back to his horse and rode off. Her gaze was on Katie. She was seeing red that Katie had let that young man touch her. Yet she couldn't take her eyes off the alabaster skin peeking from under the unhooked portion of her collar.

"He didn't do anything," Katie finally said.

"Are you always in the habit of unbuttoning your dresses when in the company of a caller?"

"Wouldn't you like to know who I unbutton my dress for?"

"I don't think it proper that you undress for anyone."

"Undress? My Lord. I unbuttoned the top few buttons because I was hot."

"I will leave you to put yourself back together." She ogled the bare skin once more before turning.

"Are you sure you wouldn't rather I unbutton a few more?"

Arousal warred with disgust as Corrine strode off, not offering a response.

❖

Katie was restless so she sought out Mollie Flanagan, the dark Irish beauty whose family were indentured servants to the Prentiss family. Mollie was twenty years old with black hair and eyes the color of dark chocolate. Katie had been sleeping with her since Mollie arrived at the plantation. Katie finally found her dusting in the upstairs hall.

Mollie smiled when she saw her approach.

"I'm bored," Katie said, still on fire from the way Miss Staples had eyed her exposed skin.

"I'm sorry to hear that," Mollie said.

"Are you?" Katie took her hand and led her into an empty guest bedroom.

"Katie, darlin,' I've got work I must see to."

"I have other things for you to see to." She lay back on the bed and hiked up her skirt, showing Mollie that she wore no underwear. "I need your mouth on me."

"Now that's mighty tempting." Mollie's eyes darkened as she gazed at the swollen, wet lips that Katie held open for her.

"Put your tongue in me," Katie said. "I'm in need."

Mollie looked saddened. "Is that an order then?"

Katie dropped her skirts and stared at Mollie.

"Oh, no, Mol. I didn't mean it like that. I'd never do that. I'm sorry. I'm just so worked up right now."

She pulled Mollie on top of her and kissed her hard, her tongue demanding entrance, and Mollie's mouth welcomed her.

Katie deftly unhooked the buttons that ran down the back of Mollie's uniform. She peeled the sleeves down her muscular arms and helped Mollie slip out of them. She folded the bodice down, revealing supple breasts begging for attention.

Katie greedily sucked the large nipples dangling over her.

"I love the sight of you suckling me."

"I love to suckle you." She flicked her tongue over one nipple then the other while she ran her hand along Mollie's leg and under her petticoat.

"What have we here?" Katie found the damp ground where Mollie's legs met. "You're wet for me already."

"Aye, but you're the one who's needy." Mollie kissed Katie again and then moved between her legs. "Let me have a go at you."

She pushed Katie's skirt out of her way and buried her tongue inside her wet slit. Katie grabbed a handful of Mollie's hair and held her in place as she bucked on the bed, wiping her juices all over Mollie's face.

She spread her legs wider to grant Mollie greater access. She shivered when she felt Mollie spread her lips and blow on her swollen clit.

"Stop," she said suddenly.

"What did I do wrong?"

"Nothing, sweetheart. I just want to get our clothes off so we can lie naked together. And I had the most delicious idea."

They climbed off the bed and kissed hungrily as they deftly removed each other's dresses. Stark naked and more aroused by the minute, Katie lay across the bed and propped herself up on some pillows.

"Why are you lying that way?"

Katie spread her legs wide but looked past Mollie as she stroked her wet cunt.

"What are you looking at?" Mollie turned and saw that Katie was watching herself in the mirror.

"Isn't that wonderful? Now climb between my legs so I can watch while your mouth's on me."

"You'll see my arse in the air. How arousing is that?"

"Very. And if you spread your legs, I'll see your cunt as well."

"I like it when you look at my cunt."

"I like it when you fuck mine."

"Well, then…" Mollie climbed on the bed and buried her tongue inside her.

Katie held back the mass of hair as she watched Mollie's head bobbing in the mirror.

"Spread your legs a little."

Mollie did as she was instructed while she took Katie's clit between her teeth and flicked her tongue over it.

"Oh, fuck yes! That feels divine." Her breath caught with every flick on her nerve center.

She fought to keep her eyes open. She was losing herself in the sensations Mollie was creating. She fondled her own breasts while she kept her focus on the mirror.

"Touch yourself."

Mollie stopped.

"Don't be a prude. Touch yourself. I want to see it in the mirror. And for God's sake, please don't stop fucking me again."

Mollie buried her tongue deep inside Katie and rubbed her nose against her slick clit. She reached her hand between her legs and stroked her own cunt for Katie.

"Oh fuck, Mollie. You have no idea how arousing that is. Oh God. Oh God. Oh dear God."

Katie felt the muscles in her belly tighten as the feelings flooded her. She closed her eyes and gave herself over to the oblivion pulling her in.

While Katie lay back and watched, Mollie climbed out from between her legs and lay next to her. Katie rolled over and kissed her.

"Thank you, sweetheart. That was just what I needed."

"Did you like that—watching me touch myself?"

"I did. Very much."

Mollie shifted to her back and let her legs fall open. She ran her fingers over her protruding clit and down to her wet cleft.

"Mollie, what you're doing to me."

"It feels so nice. I feel a bit naughty, but I'm more aroused with you watching me. I seem to enjoy it more than I ought."

"Well, don't stop."

"I couldn't if I wanted."

Katie looked at the mirror and was on fire anew at the reflection of Mollie masturbating. She moved her own hand between her legs.

"You're needing more then?"

"I can't help it. Look at us in the mirror."

They were silent as they watched each other's fingers moving frantically. Katie found herself close to climaxing again and could tell by Mollie's mewling that she was right there with her.

She tore her gaze away and rolled on her side. She closed her mouth over Mollie's nipple and sucked hard as she madly stroked her swollen clit. She shut her eyes and watched the colors explode behind her eyelids as she listened to Mollie come in unison with her.

Mollie slowly climbed out of bed. "I best get back to work before someone comes looking for me."

As they dressed, Mollie said, "That friend of your mother's, there's something about that one, isn't there?"

Katie whirled on her, not liking it one bit that Mollie might have looked at Miss Staples *that way*. "What?"

"I'm sorry, lass," Mollie said. "I didn't mean to be upsetting you. I just noticed her. And she's different."

"I'll thank you not to be mooning over my mother's guest."

"Katie?"

Katie ignored her as she stormed out, slamming the door behind her.

Chapter Four

Corrine longed to throw open the heavy black curtains and let the sun shine through the floor-to-ceiling windows in the front room. Everything was dark and heavy. She understood protocol to an extent but knew Theodore had embraced life and would be saddened by this darkness in his house.

She found Della in the glassed-in breakfast nook adjacent to the kitchen.

"How long will you keep the house closed up?"

"Until I feel ready."

"Could you not have opened them last year or even before?"

"I'm not ready, Cori."

"I'll not push you, but I have to ask myself if it's good for you or Katie to live in constant darkness."

Della sighed. "I've no idea what to do with that one."

"Katie?"

Della nodded. "I fear I've lost all control of her."

"She's a strongheaded one, to be sure."

"And I sense that she needs to get out into society, but it wouldn't do for me to attend events yet."

"It's been two years?"

"In December."

"That's darned close, Della. Do you suppose all this mourning is hurting your health?"

"There's no such thing as close, Cori. I'll mourn for two years and a day."

"And Katie?"

"Her mourning period has passed. I feel that is part of her attitude. She wants to start living again and I simply can't."

"She's young. That's understandable."

"But I'm at a loss of what to do for her."

"Perhaps it would help if I took her to the theater."

"Oh, Cori! You would do that?"

Corrine's heart skipped a beat at the thought of an evening on the town with Katie.

"If it would help, it would be my pleasure."

Della stood, tears rolling down her cheeks as she hugged her. "Oh, whatever would I do without you?"

Corrine laughed. "You shall never have to find out."

"Am I interrupting something?" Katie appeared in the doorway.

Della pulled away and wiped her eyes. "Not at all. Come here, Katie dear."

Katie looked suspiciously at Corrine as she stepped into her mother's open arms.

"Why are you crying, Mama?"

"They're happy tears, honey."

Katie wasn't convinced. "You seem to have a way of making my mother cry," she said to Corrine.

Corrine fought to keep the smile off her face.

"And you seem proud of yourself!"

The urge to smile fled. "Do you ever stop to ascertain what might be going on before you pass your judgments?"

"I bid you not to use that tone with me. You forget you hold no authority over me."

"Kathleen, please!" Della stepped away from her. "Corrine has offered to do something very nice for you, and I'll thank you to stop being so rude to her."

Katie sat at the table and glared at Corrine. "*You're* going to do something nice. For *me*?"

"That was the plan. Although I must admit to feeling as if it might not be a good idea after all. Especially since I am such a thorn in your side."

"You wouldn't be such a thorn if you'd stop making Mama cry. And if you'd act as a guest instead of my other parent."

"Kathleen!" Della said. "Miss Staples is my guest. And she's an adult. As far as I'm concerned, she's done nothing inappropriate or out of line."

"Of course you'd say that. I still say you two are conspiring against me." She looked at Corrine. "So what's this nice thing you're supposedly doing for me? And what sort of debt will that leave me in with you?"

Corrine stared hard at her, every ounce of self-discipline keeping her from lashing out. Only her love for Della kept her from rescinding her offer on the spot. She sat across from Katie. "I'll let your mother tell you. And please, feel no obligation."

Katie looked at her mother as if awaiting sentencing.

"Corrine has offered to accompany you to the theater."

Katie looked back and forth between them, her eyes sparkling. "Honestly? The theater? In New Orleans?"

"The very one." Corrine smiled at how almost childlike Katie looked.

"When? Oh, please say soon!"

"I believe I saw that someone was performing this weekend. We'll go Saturday night."

"Oh, but I've not a thing to wear! Mama, will you please take me shopping this week?"

"It wouldn't be right for me to be seen shopping. I'm sure you have plenty to wear."

"What about that satin gown you had on the day I arrived?" Corrine couldn't help but remember the exposed flesh above her shapely breasts and the way the color had brought out her eyes.

"That old thing? Why, I couldn't wear that to the theater."

"I'm sure you'll find something," Della said.

"I'd best start looking." She left the room.

"I'd be more than happy to take her shopping," Corrine said when Katie was out of earshot.

"I couldn't ask you to do that."

"You're not asking. I'm offering. And I mean it sincerely. I'll take her into town tomorrow. Shall I go tell her?"

"If you're certain. You know how she can be."

"I'm quite aware. However, I do believe I'm up for the challenge. Now if you'll excuse me."

Corrine's heart soared, and she had to deliberately take the stairs one at a time. She straightened her dressing gown, took a deep breath, and knocked on Katie's door.

"Enter."

Corrine opened the door and stood staring at the vision before her. Katie stood in front of her wardrobe, her back to Corrine. Corrine took the opportunity to stare at the way Katie's nearly sheer white nightgown clung to her shapely ass, which was obviously not covered by any undergarments. She longed to cross the room and cup that ass as she kissed Katie's neck. She imagined dropping to her knees and spinning Katie around, burying her face in the secret garden where her legs met. She knew she would smell sweet and sensual. In her mind, Katie raised the hem of her nightgown, then lowered it, trapping Corrine against her. Corrine would knead and squeeze that ass while her tongue darted between her legs.

She cleared her throat. "Katie?"

Katie spun. "Miss Staples! I'm sorry. I wasn't expecting you."

She stood with her arms at her side, obviously unaware of what the outline of her full breasts was doing to Corrine.

"I realize that. Have you had any luck?" She motioned to the open wardrobe.

"No." Katie sat hard on her bed, her breasts bouncing playfully.

Corrine forced herself not to stare. "I've actually come with good news."

"And what might that be?"

"If you have no objection, I'll be taking you into town tomorrow to shop for a new gown."

"Oh, Miss Staples." She was off the bed and in Corrine's arms before either of them had time to think.

Corrine closed her arms around her waist and held her close, breathing in the fresh scent of her youth. She shut her eyes and inhaled, her whole body alive where Katie pressed into her. She felt Katie's arms around her neck and wanted to hold her there forever.

Katie finally eased her grip. She stood, face inches from Corrine's. Corrine looked into the emerald eyes, then down to the parted pink lips practically touching hers. For the briefest of seconds, she thought about dipping to taste them, but quickly came to her senses. She stepped out of Katie's grasp.

They stood silently, and Corrine was puzzled by the blush that covered Katie from her chest up.

"Thank you so much," Katie finally said.

"You're quite welcome." Corrine straightened her dressing gown again. "I believe I'll take my leave now, if you'll excuse me."

"Of course. Thank you again."

Corrine smiled and nodded, then hurried out of the room. She leaned against the closed door and tried to steady her breathing. That had been a close call. She chastised herself and vowed not to be alone with Katie in her quarters again.

She walked down the hall on unsteady legs. She passed the beautiful young cleaning girl and smiled at her. The woman smiled knowingly at her. Corrine wondered if her encounter was written all over her face.

Heart still racing, she let herself in her room and sank onto her bed. She buried her face in her hands and cursed herself for holding Katie longer than was decent. But she'd felt so right in her arms. She'd wanted to lay her back on the bed and kiss those tender lips that were so capable of spitting venom.

She stripped out of her dressing gown and stepped in front of the mirror. She was slender and muscular, her body that of a much younger woman. She thought it worthy of the beautiful Katie. She shook her head and moved away. She wasn't thinking clearly. She quickly dressed and went back downstairs where she found Della in the sitting room.

"Della, do you know where Theodore kept his fishing gear? And would you mind if I used it?"

"Of course I don't mind. Someone might as well get use out of it. I believe he kept all his gear in a corner of the stables. He had a special bag made for it. I can't guarantee what shape it'll be in."

"I brought my own silk, so as long as he's got a pole and hooks, I should be set. I'll be gone until dinner then. And Katie was thrilled to hear about a day shopping, by the by."

"I didn't think you'd get an argument. I must say, I don't know why she's so disrespectful of you. I certainly hope she behaves tomorrow."

"Even if she does not, I promise to bring her home in one piece."

Della laughed. "Shall I plan on fish for dinner then?"

It was Corrine's turn to laugh. "I make no promise. But I shall do my best."

❖

Corrine was grateful for the solitude of the stable. She was looking forward to spending the day at the back end of the plantation with her line in the Mississippi. She was hoping the fresh air would help clear her head.

She found the saddlebag that Della had mentioned. The lancewood rod stood in three pieces next to the bag. Corrine placed them in the bag, then tucked in the silk line she'd brought with her.

She put the saddlebag on the back of the dapple mare she'd chosen and gently urged her into the sunlight and warm autumn morning. Corrine drew a deep breath but could only smell the scent of Katie's skin. It had smelled clean and fresh and young. Corrine imagined it would taste sweet and of innocence. At the thought of her innocence, her memory flew back to Katie unbuttoning her dress for that DuPre boy. She wondered how innocent Katie was. The thought that someone else may have had her made Corrine's blood boil.

She nudged the mare to speed up as she rode through the rows of tall sugar cane. The air was heavy but cooled somewhat as she reached the river. She dismounted and tied the horse to an old oak with plenty of shade but access to the river.

Corrine unpacked the saddlebag and assembled the fishing rod. She dug in the mud until she found an earthworm to run the hook through. She cast her line into the river, then sat on the cool earth.

She propped the rod on a branch she stuck in the ground, then lay back using the saddlebag as a pillow and let the warmth take her cares away.

❖

Katie sat on her bed reliving every second of the hug. Miss Staples's arms were strong and sure as they'd held her. She still had gooseflesh where Miss Staples's warm breath caressed her bare skin. Her nipples were taut and painful as she craved more. Then there was the look in her deep blue eyes when they stared into hers. Was it her imagination or had she seen desire there? Katie was certain Miss Staples had come close to kissing her. She could just imagine her kiss, firm and possessive.

She sighed. She determined to strive to give Miss Staples every opportunity to kiss her. She simply had to discover what that kiss would be like. She slipped a housecoat over her nightgown and left her room.

Katie saw Mollie coming out of Miss Staples's room.

"What were you doing in there?" she said.

"Katie, are you speaking to me now?"

"Answer me. What were you doing in there?"

"I was cleaning, of course."

"Is she in there?"

"No. She doesn't like me to clean when she's in. Now will you tell me what I did to upset you so yesterday?"

"I don't like hearing that you're attracted to Miss Staples."

"Kathleen Prentiss! Are you jealous?"

Very, Katie thought. *But not how you think.*

"Maybe a little," she said. "Hey, I have an idea." She took Mollie's hand and pulled her into Miss Staples's room where she threw her on the bed and climbed on top. She kissed her hard on her mouth, her tongue forcing Mollie's mouth open. Her breath caught when their tongues met and she felt her clit growing. She took one of Mollie's hands and put it between her legs.

"Oh, Katie, you know I can't say no to you."

"That's what I'm counting on." She grinned.

"But what if she comes in?"

"Maybe she'll join us."

"Katie! I'm shocked at you." She pulled her hand out. "I'm not sure about this."

Katie moved to straddle Mollie's belly. She took off her housecoat and pulled her gown over her head. She began playing with her breasts.

"Katie, I'm serious. How would it look to be caught like this?"

Katie paid her no heed. She leaned back on one hand and slipped her other hand between them so Mollie could watch her touch herself.

"Your clit is so big," Mollie said as she watched Katie masturbate on top of her.

"It feels amazing," she murmured. She was so aroused by fucking in Miss Staples's room. Part of her wished Miss Staples would come in and take over for her.

"You look amazing, but you're getting my dress all wet."

"You'll smell me all day. Won't that be a treat?"

Katie walked up her body on her knees and sat on Mollie's face, grinding into her, and Mollie slid her tongue inside. She writhed over her face, amazed at the height of her arousal.

"Suck me then," she begged, and Mollie obliged. Katie could hold out no longer. She threw her head back and cried out as a powerful orgasm tore through her.

She moved off the bed and smiled down at Mollie. "Now you'll taste me all day, as well as smell me."

"That will be a treat indeed."

"Now you take your clothes off and let me at you."

"I wish I could. I've got to get back to cleaning. My mum will be up here to fetch me for lunch soon. It wouldn't do for her to find us like that."

"I don't suppose it would." Katie laughed. "Well, this was fun. We'll have to fuck in here again."

"Maybe when my heart starts beating normally. Now let's get out of this room before she comes in."

Chapter Five

Corrine sipped a cup of chicory while she pored over the plantation's books. Something wasn't right. She'd thought she'd seen a discrepancy Monday, which was another reason she'd taken the previous day off. She'd run through the numbers in her mind while she was out by the river, and no matter how she ran them, something wasn't right. Money was missing.

"Miss Staples. You're not dressed yet?"

She turned, and her breath caught at the sight of Katie in a long russet gown that accented her soft auburn hair and made her eyes sparkle.

Corrine stood and stared. "Katie," she began. "I...you..."

Katie smiled as if she knew the effect she was having.

Corrine cleared her throat. "What I'm trying to say is that you look beautiful."

"Thank you." Katie curtsied, then her eyes hardened. "I wish I could say the same for you. We need to get to town and you're still lounging about."

Corrine grinned. "I'm hardly lounging about. I've been looking over the books since early this morning so I'd be able to go to town. I didn't realize how late it'd gotten. If you'll excuse me, I'll go change and will be back promptly."

She brushed against Katie as she walked around her to take her leave. Every nerve in her body was alive.

❖

Katie sat in her father's chair to wait for Miss Staples to return. She missed her father and felt the familiar resentment toward Miss Staples for trying to take his place. She knew her mother hadn't known anything about keeping books when he'd been killed, but Mollie's father had been helping. She didn't understand why her mother had called on Miss Staples to come look at them.

She told herself she would ask Miss Staples to teach her about the books. Not that accounting sounded very interesting to her, but it would make her feel closer to her father. And it would allow her to be more involved in the plantation. She made up her mind. She would mention it to Miss Staples.

"I didn't expect to find you still here," Corrine said from the doorway.

"Do you think I could learn the books?" Katie asked without turning around.

Corrine crossed the room and stood next to Katie. She placed her finger under her chin and forced her to look her in the eyes.

"Is that a serious question? Because that's not very ladylike."

"You're a fine one to talk."

She moved her hand. "It's not my place to pass judgment. I simply reminded you."

"But you took over your father's business when he died. How old were you?"

"I was twenty-seven. Running a plantation entails more than simply keeping books."

"But it's a place to start, yes?"

"That it is. Now, lovely lady, shall we depart? The coach awaits." She offered her elbow, and Katie placed her hand around it.

They walked to the breakfast nook to bid farewell to Della, then Corrine escorted Katie to the waiting coach. She held the door for her, then climbed in after. She sat across from her and once again smiled at how beautiful Katie looked.

"That dress is really very beautiful. I fail to see that you need any other piece of clothing. You should always wear that."

Katie blushed and Corrine had to look away, lest Katie see the desire in her eyes.

The ride passed quickly, mostly in silence.

"Where shall I drop you?" the driver called over his shoulder.

"In front of Franklin's Dry Goods," Corrine replied.

The driver pulled the coach in front of the large store on Canal Street. Corrine stepped out of the coach and held the door for Katie, who was beaming in anticipation of her day.

Katie threw her arms around Corrine. "I can't believe we're here. It's been so long."

Corrine barely heard her. She was aware of little save the feel of Katie's breasts pressed into her.

"Come now." She disentangled herself. "Let's go see what we can find for you."

Katie grabbed her hand and pulled her into the giant emporium. The store was the size of a city block and teemed with crowds. Katie had barely entered the store when she was pulled into one hug after another from squealing young women, apparently thrilled to see her.

Corrine stood back and simply observed. It pleased her to see Katie so in her element. It reinforced to her that age was not their only difference. Corrine was fine on the docks with the workers milling about, but she was decidedly out of her element in the store with the fancily attired gentlefolk. And it appeared to be where Katie flourished.

Katie excused herself from a group she had been talking to and walked to Corrine. "People think I'm unaccompanied."

"I'm sure they know your mother would never allow that. I'm keeping an eye on you. I can't imagine you'd want me hovering over you."

"Well, I just wanted to say if you would be more comfortable hovering, as you say, I'd be fine with that."

"I assure you, I'm fine leaving you to the limelight."

"Isn't it just wonderful?" Katie fairly squealed. "Doesn't everyone look beautiful? Oh, how I've missed this. And they all say how wonderful I look. It's as if I'm dreaming."

Corrine had to smile at her. "I'm thrilled you're enjoying yourself so."

Katie took her hand. It felt soft and warm. Corrine cringed at her impure thoughts.

"Let's walk toward the material room. Anyone who's anyone will be there."

"The material room?"

"Yes. See the high ceiling?" She motioned to the center of the store.

Corrine saw the two-story gothic vaulted ceiling. "What's there?"

"It's where all the material is kept, silly. I want to find the perfect color and feel for Saturday. Then we'll choose a pattern and a seamstress."

They jostled their way through the crowds, often being pressed into each other. More than once, Corrine's hand ended up on Katie's derriere.

She found herself blushing and apologizing the whole way to the material room. Katie seemed undisturbed.

If Corrine thought the entrance to the emporium was crowded, there was no word to describe the material room in the center of the store. Girls shrieked in excitement at everything—the sight of long-lost friends, the feel of the perfect material, even finding the perfect pattern. Corrine felt a headache beginning at her temples.

She briefly lost Katie in the crowd but soon found her, as no one else could compare to her beauty. She recognized her from her long, shining hair and the tilt of her head when she laughed. She walked over to find her surrounded by a group of young women, all obviously thrilled to be in her presence.

Katie looked like she was holding court. Corrine tried to retreat, but Katie reached out and took her hand again.

"Everyone, this is my mother's dearest friend, Miss Staples. Miss Staples, these are all girls who went to finishing school with me."

"It's a pleasure to meet you all." Corrine smiled easily. It was wonderful to see how Katie glowed.

The girls all looked at her with questions in their gazes. Corrine knew Katie would be the subject of many whispers for being seen with a woman in trousers. She wondered if she'd considered that. She found it hard to believe that Katie did anything that wasn't carefully calculated.

"Don't her trousers look comfortable?" Katie was saying. Corrine choked back a laugh. "I'm thinking of having a pair made."

The girls didn't try to hide their shock.

"Katie!" one of them exclaimed. "It's not right."

"Well, I think it should be all right. Aren't they comfortable, Miss Staples?"

Corrine looked at her, amused. "Why, yes. They are quite comfortable."

"Why shouldn't more of us wear them?" Katie asked.

The girls looked at her as if she'd lost her mind. They slowly backed away.

Katie broke into laughter. "Wasn't that wonderful?"

"You are a riddle, Katie Prentiss."

"Oh, they are all too prim for their own good."

"And I fear you may not be prim enough for yours."

"Oh, Miss Staples, please, let's not fight today."

"Fair enough. Have you looked at any material yet?"

"Not yet. Look around. Isn't it amazing? Look at all the choices."

Corrine finally allowed her focus to wander from Katie. She saw rows and rows of shelves filled with every type of material in every color of the rainbow and then some.

"Come help me choose."

"Oh, this really isn't my forte."

"But you must help me. Here, this is what we'll do. I'll hand you a swatch, or you can find one and we'll hold it under my chin, like this." She grabbed a light blue swatch and demonstrated.

"How does this look?"

Corrine felt foolish but fought to overcome it to make Katie's day special. "It looks stunning."

Katie blushed. "Okay, then hold this one. Now you choose a swatch."

Corrine knew she was out of her element but couldn't tell if Katie was toying with her or truly wanting her assistance. She had no choice but to go along with her, so she grabbed a rust-colored swatch.

"Now hold it under my chin." She tilted her head back slightly. The color complemented her eyes.

Corrine took a few strands of Katie's hair and laid them over the swatch. "It's a nice color too. But I don't like it with your hair."

"I could have told you that." She smiled. "So choose another color. Anything but black. I simply couldn't bear wearing black."

Corrine turned this way and that, trying to find the perfect color. She was relieved when Katie decided to help. Katie reached around her, pressing her bosom into Corrine's back. She stiffened, even as she felt her crotch clench.

Katie placed her hand in the middle of Corrine's back. "You need to learn to relax, Miss Staples."

"I suppose you're right."

Katie spun her around after she grabbed the swatch. Corrine was trapped between Katie and the shelves. Katie stood inches from her.

"What do you think of this color?"

Corrine swallowed hard and tried to stay focused on the task at hand. Katie was holding a hunter green swatch. Corrine was amazed at the way her eyes sparkled and the accents in her hair shone. Even her soft pink lips seemed lovelier with the swatch held near.

"Miss Staples?"

"I apologize, Katie. But that color is simply stunning. Your dress must be that color."

Katie hugged her. "Thank you for playing along." She kissed her cheek, then stepped back.

"Well," Corrine began. "I suppose I didn't realize how important this was to you."

"It really does mean the world to me."

"Now then, what's next?"

"Now we go look at patterns. We need to find the perfect gown."

"And what will that look like?"

"Silly, I won't know until I see it."

"Surely you have some idea."

"Do you really want to know?"

"Of course. Tell me." Corrine couldn't wipe the smile off her face. Katie's excitement was contagious. The kiss hadn't hurt.

Katie stopped walking and traced the outline of her imaginary dress. "The bodice will dip to here." She pointed to the crevice between her breasts. "I want puffy sleeves that come to just above my elbow. Oh, it'll be beautiful."

"Sounds wonderful," Corrine managed, her mind's eye still envisioning Katie's cleavage in the dress.

They arrived at a table covered in books with likenesses of dresses drawn in them. Katie sat and patted the chair next to her. She slid a book over to Corrine. "Help me look."

Katie flipped through her book and reached for another. Corrine was staring at a picture in her book. The sleeves weren't terribly puffy, but she couldn't stop looking at the picture, imagining Katie in the low-cut bodice. Moisture pooled between her legs. She knew it was a dangerous thought and was about to close the book when Katie cried out next to her.

"That's it! That's the perfect dress!"

"Katie, don't you think that might be a little…mature for you?"

"I'm not a child, Miss Staples. That is my dream dress. Carry the book for me?"

"Where are we off to now?" Corrine heard herself ask when she knew she should have argued the inappropriateness of the dress.

"We need to go to one of the measuring rooms. Those are in the back. Come on."

She led Corrine to a bank of doors along the outer wall at the rear of the store. Several doors were open, and Katie stopped at a desk in front of one.

"Good afternoon." A woman with a kind face looked up at her. "How may I help you?"

"I'm going to need a dress made by Friday."

The woman raised her eyebrows. "That's a tall order."

Corrine stepped forward. "I'm prepared to pay for the rush."

"Please. You must have a seamstress available." Katie was near tears.

"One moment please." She walked away from her station and spoke to a group of women seated in the corner.

"Oh, I hope they can do this."

"I'm sure they will." Corrine had already decided no amount of money would be too much to pay for Katie's happiness.

"They won't say no to you, will they?" Katie pleaded with her eyes. "You'll intimidate them, I'm certain."

Corrine wasn't sure how to take that. "I don't like to threaten people if that's what you mean."

Katie cocked her head and looked at her. "Not threaten, really, but you are an imposing figure."

"I'm not sure whether to be insulted." Corrine was tired. Tired of shopping, tired of being aroused all day, and not sure she could keep from being baited by Katie.

"Not insulted at all. I'm just quite certain women don't usually say no to you."

Before Corrine could ask what that was supposed to mean, the woman was back with a younger woman in tow.

"Hello." The younger woman with frizzy blond hair held her hand out to Katie. "My name is Addie."

"Nice to meet you," Katie said. "I'm Katie Prentiss, and this is my mother's friend, Miss Staples."

Corrine shook her hand and didn't miss the appreciative, lingering gaze that ran from her head to her toes and back.

"Very nice to meet you, Miss Staples. Perhaps while you're here, we could fit you for a new pair of trousers?"

"We're here for a dress," Katie said, her displeasure apparent.

Corrine had to look away to hide her smile, knowing that Katie was jealous. The idea sent her heart soaring.

"Of course. What dress are you looking at?"

Corrine turned back around and handed the book to Addie and let Katie flip through it to find the correct page.

"That's beautiful. Oh, it's perfect for you. And what will we be making it out of?"

Katie handed her the swatch of the dark green. "I'd like this made from satin."

"Of course. This will be a joy to make. Come on in and let's get you measured."

Corrine watched their retreating backs and stood awkwardly, unsure of whether to join them. She was decidedly uncomfortable not knowing what to expect in the other room.

"Miss Staples," Katie called to her. "Aren't you coming in?"

"Surely I can find a place to wait out here."

"We have a table and chairs in here. You'll be comfortable," Addie said. When Corrine entered the room, Addie laughed. "Besides, you just might enjoy this."

Corrine felt less comfortable than before. She took in the room that was approximately the size of her room at the plantation. In the center was a platform a few steps high. Immediately to her left were a table and chairs. She sat down to await what was next.

Katie climbed onto the platform. Corrine watched in dismay when Addie began unbuttoning the buttons on the back of her dress. Her stomach turned when Addie winked at her. She wanted to tear her away from Katie and undress her herself. This was Addie's job. She shouldn't enjoy undressing Katie that much.

Her comfort lessened greatly when Katie peeled her sleeves off and stepped out of the dress. She stood there in her sheer cotton chemise under her corset. Her full breasts rested on the top of her white corset, her nipples hard against the flimsy material of her chemise. Corrine knew she was staring but couldn't stop until Katie ran her hands over her breasts.

Corrine looked into her eyes, which twinkled playfully. Katie ran her hands down her sides, then moved them behind to cup her ass. Corrine stared at the patch of auburn hair visible under the chemise. She wanted to drop to her knees in front of her and lick her cunt until she begged her to stop. She tore her gaze away.

Addie handed Corrine the dress. "Bet you wish you had my job, eh?"

"That's enough out of you," Corrine said, lowering her voice when she saw Katie looking at her questioningly. "It would do you well to pay attention to your job and keep your filthy mind off her."

"Can I be blamed for loving my job?"

Addie climbed onto the platform with Katie. She squatted and held one end of the tape measure at Katie's ankle. She looked up, and Corrine knew exactly what she was looking at. She was rapidly losing her patience.

"Did you want to help me then?" Addie asked her. Corrine thought the woman was much stronger than she would have been. She wouldn't be able to look at Katie's hidden treasure without touching it.

Corrine made a show of removing her pocket watch. "How much longer is this going to take?"

"I'm in no hurry. Are you, lass?" Addie asked.

"Miss Staples, please. I want to make sure everything is measured correctly. I want the dress to be perfect."

Corrine was torn. She didn't trust herself around Addie. She ached to take her fists to her. She knew Katie would never forgive her. She thought about waiting elsewhere but didn't want to leave Katie alone with Addie. So she sat watching and throbbing all over.

Addie made notes as she measured ankle to waist and elbow to shoulder. She enjoyed measuring Katie's bustline too much for Corrine's taste. She didn't need to measure from the front, but Corrine knew she wanted the excuse to rub against her tits. She seethed.

Corrine thought her head would explode when Addie held one end of the tape at the base of Katie's neck and held the other in her hand that disappeared under her chemise between her breasts. When she finally finished, Corrine stood and strode to Katie with her dress.

She held her hand up and Katie took it and allowed her to help her down the steps and off the platform. Corrine handed Katie her dress.

"The dress will be ready Friday afternoon?" she asked Addie while Katie dressed.

"Yes, ma'am."

"We'll be back then to try it on. Thank you for everything. I'll see you out there," she said to Katie and stepped out of the dressing room.

She found the same woman sitting at the desk and quickly approached her. "Excuse me. We'll be back Friday to try on the dress Miss Prentiss was just fitted for."

"Of course."

She handed the woman a dollar bill. "I would appreciate it if Addie not be the one to assist us that day."

Katie walked up to see the woman slip the bill in her bodice. "Anything you'd like, ma'am. She won't bother you Friday."

"What was that about?"

"Nothing you need to worry your pretty head about. Are you at all hungry?"

"I'm famished."

"Then would you be kind enough to accompany me to dinner?"

Katie beamed. "It would be my pleasure."

Corrine offered her elbow. "Shall we?"

Katie rested her hand inside Corrine's elbow as they cut through the back of the store in search of a restaurant.

CHAPTER SIX

They strolled along Dumaine Street, down to Decatur, to Bon Mange, a French restaurant overlooking the river. Corrine reveled in the closeness of Katie and cared little about the stares from passersby.

"You didn't like Addie, did you?" Katie asked.

Corrine weighed her answer carefully. "It's true I didn't like her unsavory thoughts about you."

"Have you ever had an unsavory thought, Miss Staples?" Katie said.

"If I had, I would certainly not discuss them in the company of a lady."

"You sound like that inane Thomas DuPre."

Corrine tensed. "I fear you need not remind me who he is."

"Thank you for trying to protect me from him." Katie held Corrine's arm and pressed her breast into it.

Heat coursed through Corrine's body. The feel of Katie against her warred with the anger at what Katie had let Thomas do, threatening to impede her ability to reason.

"I'd rather not ruin a lovely evening with talk of that incident."

"Have you ever been in love, Miss Staples?"

The question caught Corrine off guard. "Why, yes, I believe I have."

"What was it like?"

Corrine laughed. "Horrible."

"Why?" Katie stopped and stared into her eyes.

"Mostly the struggle of wanting her so badly and not being able to have her."

"So she didn't love you back then."

"Unfortunately, she did not."

"She was a fool," Katie said softly and turned to enter the restaurant.

The restaurant was crowded but not so much that Corrine and Katie had to wait. The host led them past booths carved of rich cypress to a table in the corner.

"This place is beautiful," Katie said.

"I'm glad you like it." Corrine was bursting inside that she was impressing Katie.

The waiter arrived and listed the fare for the evening.

"That sounds perfect," Corrine said. "We'll also have a carafe of Meursault."

"As you wish." The waiter bowed and backed away.

"The menu sounds delicious. How did you find this place?"

"Your parents and I used to come here when you were a child. Your aunt would sit with you while I treated them to a nice dinner."

"Do you miss me as a child?"

"Do you miss being a child?"

"Not at all. But I still think you preferred me as a child."

The waiter was back with their wine. Corrine handed a glass to Katie, then took a sip of hers.

"When you were a child, I couldn't have treated you to the day we had today, could I?"

"So you must not hate me then to have done this for me."

"I most certainly do not hate you. Quite the contrary."

Katie smiled as she set her wine glass down.

"Now let me turn the question around," Corrine said. "Did you like me more when you were a child or now?"

"We had so much fun together when I was little. But today was the best. I think we can have a different kind of relationship now that I'm older."

Corrine was grateful that the waiter had appeared with their food. Every ounce of her being wanted to ask what sort of relationship Katie might want with her. Every ounce of her being was terrified of the answer.

After dinner, they walked back to Franklin's and found their carriage waiting for them. Corrine helped Katie up and climbed in after her.

"Won't you sit down?" she asked.

"After you," Katie said.

"That's rather unusual for me. Is there a reason you won't sit first?"

"If I do, you'll sit across from me."

"Is that an issue?"

"I want to sit next to you."

Corrine smiled. "That can be arranged. Please have a seat."

Katie sat and Corrine sat next to her. Katie rested her head on Corrine's shoulder.

Corrine resisted the urge to put her arm around Katie's shoulders. Instead, she made herself as comfortable as she'd allow and simply enjoyed Katie's nearness.

As the coach moved down the road, Katie looked up at Corrine.

"Do you know much about the upcoming election?"

"Oh, Katie. You don't want to discuss that."

"I do. But no one else takes me seriously enough to talk to me about it. You will, though, won't you?"

"What does a young lady such as yourself care of such a dull subject as politics?"

"I hear things. I hear slaves talking, saying they'll be free if this Lincoln is elected. Is this true? Nobody will tell me what's going on."

Corrine sighed. "I'll tell you what I've heard. This Lincoln character believes Negroes should be relocated to other countries, that they don't belong as property in this country."

"I hope he doesn't win. Our lives would be completely upended, wouldn't they? Would we lose the plantation? What would Mama and I do?"

A tear spilled from Katie's eye. Corrine wiped it away. "Please let's talk about something more pleasant. Let's not tarnish this wonderful day."

"I'm grateful to you, Miss Staples. Thank you for caring enough about me to talk to me about this."

"I'd like never to deny you anything."

Katie smiled. "I'd like that too."

With Katie's face turned up to hers, Corrine once again found those soft lips just inches away. She moved her gaze to Katie's eyes. Her breath caught at the raw desire she saw there. She looked away just as Katie leaned into her. Katie's lips met her cheek.

"That's two kisses in one day," Corrine tried to joke. "I'm beginning to think you don't hate me, either."

"Quite the contrary," Katie said under her breath as she settled in against her for the rest of the ride.

Della was waiting for them in the living room when they got home.

"Oh, Mama!" Katie cried as she sat next to her on the sofa. "We had the most marvelous day, didn't we, Miss Staples?"

Corrine stood there, hands in her pockets and a smile on her face. "That we did, Katie."

"I found the perfect dress. It's dark green and satin, and we get to pick it up Friday. I'm so excited."

"I'm so happy to hear y'all had a good day." Della looked at Corrine. "So there were no problems at all?"

"Of course not," Katie continued to gush. "And Miss Staples took me to the most marvelous restaurant that had the best shrimp remoulade. We even drank wine."

Della raised her eyebrows at Corrine. "You did, did you?"

"The whole day was magical, Mama." She kissed Della's cheek. "I'm going to go upstairs and get ready for bed. Good night."

She stood and wrapped her arms around Corrine's neck. "Thank you again."

Corrine stepped back. "Good night, Katie."

They watched Katie go up the stairs. Della finally spoke. "She's like a different child."

Corrine collapsed on a chair across from her. "She was like a different person all day. She seemed to enjoy herself very much. I hope it helps her attitude. I honestly hope I didn't just create a monster, though."

"How so?"

"I worry she'll only be happy on days like today and expect them more often."

Della laughed. "I'm sure she knows these are special treats and won't happen every day." She grew serious. "Have you found anything from reviewing the books?"

Corrine leaned forward and rested her elbows on her knees. "I'm glad you had me come when your allowance was short again this month. There's no reason for plantation profits to be so much less as of late. Something isn't right. I haven't found where it went off, but things aren't adding up."

"Who would be taking money from me?"

Corrine shook her head. "I plan to go back to the last day Theodore touched the books and work my way forward until I find it."

"I'm sure Paddy Flanagan will be happy to assist you. He took over when Theodore left."

"Who's Paddy and why did Theodore choose him?"

"Paddy is an indentured servant. No doubt you've seen his daughter, Mollie, cleaning around the house."

"I know of the girl. How was Paddy chosen?"

"He kept books for a potato farmer in Ireland. It made sense for him to take over while Theodore was gone."

"How did he come to be in your service?"

"Theodore paid his family's passage to New Orleans a few years ago."

Corrine stood. "I'll certainly seek Paddy out if I need to. Now if you'll excuse me, I'm off to retire for the night."

"Good night, Cori."

"One more thing. Katie mentioned a desire to learn the books. I thought I ought to mention that to you."

"I honestly don't know what that girl thinks sometimes."

Corrine shook her head and climbed the stairs to her room.

❖

Corrine was deep in thought when Katie walked into the office wearing a light blue wrapper over her nightgown. "Did you start without me?"

Corrine started. "I wasn't expecting you."

"Honestly, you must learn to take me seriously."

Gone was the tender woman-child from the day before. In her place was the obnoxious young woman with no regard for anyone but herself.

"Did you speak with your mother?"

"Why would I speak with her?"

Della walked up. "Because I'm your mother."

Katie rolled her eyes but kept her back to Della. "I need to have something to do with running this place. I see nothing wrong with learning to keep the books."

Corrine couldn't have been less comfortable. "Excuse me." She stood.

"You don't need to leave, Miss Staples. Lessons should begin now."

"I disagree, Katie. I do need to leave. You need to discuss this with your mother. I'll not be put in the middle of this."

Katie watched Corrine walk out and wanted to scream at her to stay. She wanted to spend time with her at any cost. The day before had been heavenly. Everything had been right. She thought they were moving forward, but now she felt like she was being treated like a child again.

She finally looked at her mother. "Go ahead. Tell me why I can't do this."

"It's not whether you can or can't."

"It's whether it's proper or not. I know."

"No, it's a matter of you asking my permission. Those books control the success or failure of this plantation. That's a lot of responsibility. This place was your father's dream. I'm insulted that you care so little about that that you wouldn't consult me about something like this. Add to that, we are finding money missing. Even if I approved of you doing this, now isn't a good time for you to begin."

Katie stared at her. "Money is missing? How did that happen?"

"That's what Miss Staples is here to find out."

Katie stepped forward and took her mother's hands. "Please, Mama. Now I'm more determined than ever to learn this. Please let me help Miss Staples find out what's going on. Please. For Daddy?"

Her mother stared hard at her, clearly weighing her options. "I wish I'd learned to say no to you when you were younger. I'll allow you to sit with Miss Staples. But only if you stay out of her way when she tells you to. If she has time to instruct you, fine. But if she's too busy, you'll leave her be until she has time. Is that understood?"

"Thank you, Mama!" She threw her arms around her and held her tight. "You're the best mother ever! I'm going to go find Miss Staples and tell her."

She hurried out of the room and walked through the downstairs looking for Corrine. When she couldn't find her, she walked onto the porch and saw her in a rocking chair. She looked so peaceful with her eyes closed and her hands crossed over her stomach.

She approached her quietly. "Miss Staples?"

Corrine opened an eye, then sat up. "Katie. How did the talk with your mother go?"

Katie sat in a rocker next to her. "Who's stealing from us?"

"She told you that?"

Katie nodded.

"I don't know what's going on. I've much more research to do before I can determine when money started disappearing."

Katie stood. "Well then, we should get started."

"Your mother approved?"

"Of course." Katie smiled. "But she said I can't get in your way. You'll let me know if I'm in the way, won't you?"

"I will. But will you listen?"

"I promise I'll try."

Corrine laughed. "I suppose that's all one can ever ask of you, isn't it?"

She stood and hugged Katie to her. Katie ran her arms around her neck, her breath warm on Corrine's skin.

"Well, I see you two are ready to work together." Della laughed.

Corrine immediately stepped back and cleared her throat. She felt the blush on her ears and wondered if her feelings for Katie were as obvious as they felt.

"We are," Katie said. She grabbed Corrine's hand and dragged her back to the office.

❖

Corrine pulled an extra chair up to the desk so Katie could sit next to her and see what she was explaining. She felt Katie's presence like the heat from a raging fire. Katie leaned over her to see everything Corrine explained. Her breasts rubbed against Corrine's arm as she peered closer to the books to decipher her father's chicken scratch.

Corrine told herself Katie would lose interest in a couple of hours, but such was not the case. She proved herself a quick study. She easily grasped which column indicated money going out versus goods being sold and money coming in. By the end of the day, Corrine had given her a book to look over by herself to see if she found anything out of line.

When Della came in to get them for dinner, Katie was still in her wrapper and Corrine in her dressing gown.

"You two have been quiet all day. Somehow I thought I'd hear yelling or more coming from this room."

"I'm very proud of her," Corrine said. "She's very sharp. The only bad thing to report is we still haven't found where the money started disappearing."

"We will, though," Katie said. "I'm starving. We should change for dinner."

Corrine let herself into her room and quickly dressed for dinner.

❖

Katie left Corrine at her room and continued down the hall to hers. She found Mollie dusting in her room.

"Now this is a pleasant surprise." She sidled up behind her and caressed Mollie's crotch.

"Katie! What has gotten into you?" Mollie spun around to face her. "Where have you been all day? You're not even dressed yet, and it's nigh on nightfall."

"Oh, Mollie! I'm learning bookkeeping. It's so interesting."

"I thought your mum's friend was doing the books."

"She's teaching me. It's been a great day." She dropped her robe and took her nightgown off over her head.

"What would someone say if they walked in right now?"

"It's not like I'm fucking you. I'm just changing clothes. But as long as you're here." She kissed Mollie hard, forcing her tongue in her mouth.

Mollie kissed her back with equal passion and ran her hands over Katie's naked curves. Katie's nipples hardened at her touch. Her cunt dripped with need.

"You'd better leave or I will have to fuck you," Katie said.

Corrine left her room just in time to see Mollie leaving Katie's. She swore her lips were swollen and her face flushed. Jealousy washed over her. She needed to gain control of herself before she went downstairs. As she turned to go back into her room to collect herself, Katie came out of her room. Her face lit up at the sight of Corrine.

"Perfect timing."

"So it would seem." Corrine stared hard to see if she was flushed, too, but noted nothing.

"What are you doing? Why are you looking at me that way?"

"No reason. Just enjoying your beauty."

"I declare, Miss Staples, you do good things for a girl's ego."

Chapter Seven

Corrine climbed out of her hot bath and dried slowly, trying to calm her nerves. She felt like a teenager preparing to call on her sweetheart for the first time. She applied powder to her underarms and chest, which were already beading with perspiration.

She brushed her hair until it was soft. She closed her eyes and imagined Katie's fingers moving through her hair. She opened her eyes and shook her head. She was doing Della a favor. She needed to get rid of her impure thoughts. She was having second thoughts about taking Katie to see *Romeo and Juliet*. It would be painful to watch a tale of forbidden love while sitting with hers.

She carefully removed her clothes from her wardrobe. She slid on her black linen slacks, white shirt, gray vest, and burgundy jacket. She studied herself in the mirror as she smoothed away imaginary wrinkles. When she had wasted as much time as possible, she checked her pocket watch. They still had a half hour before they needed to leave. She went downstairs and joined Della in the sitting room.

"You look quite dapper, Cori."

"Thank you. I do enjoy dressing for the theater."

"Do you know anything about the troupe that's performing?"

"I've heard only bits about Miss Kate Reignolds, who plays Juliet, but I've heard rave reviews about the lead, a Mr. J. Wilkes Booth. He's supposed to be a phenomenal tragedian. I've wanted to see him perform for years now."

"Well, we have to pull for a great show now, don't we?"

Corrine heard a door close upstairs and turned her attention to the top of the stairs. She was rewarded momentarily when Katie appeared, a vision in her deep green dress that barely covered her breasts and clung to her waist before flaring and flowing to the floor.

Della turned to see what had Corrine's attention. She stared at Katie, then back to Corrine.

"Doesn't she look beautiful?" Corrine asked, not taking her eyes off Katie as she appeared to float down the stairs.

"She looks awfully mature. Are you certain that dress is appropriate for public?"

"Apparently, it's all the rage. And she is nineteen, after all."

Katie reached the bottom of the stairs. She looked from Corrine to her mother. "Do either of you have anything to say to *me*?"

Corrine opened her mouth, but nothing came out. Della wiped a tear away and rushed to hug Katie. "My baby has grown up."

Katie hugged her mother back but kept her gaze on Corrine, who finally spoke.

"You look ravishing, Katie. You'll no doubt be the belle of the ball."

"Thank you, Miss Staples." She curtsied. "And you look most handsome. That coat makes your eyes a deep blue. It's very flattering."

Corrine felt the color rush to her cheeks. She hadn't blushed in years, but Katie Prentiss turned her inside out. Her reactions to Katie no longer surprised her.

"Why, thank you." She bowed to Katie. When she stood, she reached out a hand. "Shall we?"

"How late will you be?" Della asked.

Corrine had forgotten she was there. She cleared her throat. "We'll be having dinner after, so I imagine it'll be quite late."

"Then I won't wait up for you. Have a wonderful time, and I want to hear all about it in the morning."

❖

Corrine had hired an enclosed coach for the evening and was not disappointed in her decision. When they arrived, the driver opened the door for them, and when Katie stepped onto Camp Street, traffic came to a standstill. Men and women alike stopped to admire the beautiful Katie. Corrine beamed with pride as she took her on her arm to escort her into the theater.

"We studied *Romeo and Juliet* in finishing school," Katie said when they were seated. "It's such a sad story."

"Some people simply aren't meant to be together," Corrine said ruefully.

"Nonsense. I believe in happily ever afters."

"You are young, aren't you?"

"And you are cynical." She laughed and rested her head on Corrine's shoulder.

The play was well performed, and Corrine was beside herself with Katie's reactions. She buried her face in Corrine's lapel when Romeo drank the poison and borrowed her handkerchief when Juliet stabbed herself.

They followed the crowd into the street where the evening had cooled pleasantly. Katie took Corrine's arm, and they strolled down Canal Street to Lafitte's, a fine restaurant known for its seafood.

Corrine was thankful they were able to get a table, as the place was overrun with theatergoers. While the restaurant was loud, their table in the corner was secluded from the crowds. They sipped their chardonnay as they relaxed and enjoyed their meal.

"Thank you again for taking me out tonight. That play was magnificent."

"I was happy to get to see the lead, Mr. Booth. I've heard wonderful things about him."

"He did so well. He and the woman who was Juliet were so believable." Katie sighed. "A great play but so sad a tale."

"I enjoyed seeing it with you," Corrine said.

"Really?" Katie smiled. "Why might that be?"

"Because you reacted so completely to every part. I loved watching you watch it."

Katie blushed. "You make me feel foolish. Can I help it I enjoyed it so?"

"No need to feel foolish. I mean it. It was a treat."

When dinner was finished and the last of the wine consumed, Katie declared, "I don't want this evening to end."

Corrine looked at her. Katie had transformed from incorrigible teen to mature woman over the past few days, and that only made it harder for Corrine not to act on her feelings.

"I'm pleased you've enjoyed yourself."

When they were back in the carriage heading home, Katie snuggled up against Corrine.

"Do you love my mother, Miss Staples?"

"Why would you ask such a thing?"

"Because I'd like to know. Do you love her?"

"Very much."

"How?"

"What? Oh, no, Katie. Not like that. Never like that. She's been my best friend since we were schoolchildren."

Katie looked up at Corrine, her face inches away. "Would you ever hurt her?"

"I know you've seen me make her cry, but I assure you, I'd never intentionally hurt your mother."

"I wasn't thinking of that at all. But what if there was something you wanted to do but knew it would hurt her if she found out? Would you do it?"

Corrine was dizzy from the feel of Katie's breath on her cheek. She could think of no example of doing anything to hurt Della save making love with Katie, and she was sure Katie wasn't talking about that.

"I can't imagine such a conundrum," she said.

It was Katie who closed the distance between their mouths and tenderly brushed Corrine's lips with her own.

Corrine's first response was to pull away, but Katie was insistent. Corrine soon melted into the kiss, and after several minutes, she finally pressed her tongue against Katie's lips. Katie opened them, and Corrine moaned as their tongues met, sending flames throughout her body.

She dared to place her hands in Katie's silky hair and run her fingers through it. She held Katie's mouth to hers as their kiss deepened. She felt Katie's hands on her lapels, pulling her closer, and she needed to feel more.

Corrine disentangled her hands from Katie's long hair and deftly removed her coat and unbuttoned her vest. Katie's hands went to her chest, caressing just above where her aching breasts were pleading for contact.

Corrine moved her mouth from Katie's and softly nibbled her exposed neck. Her skin was soft and tasted sweeter even than she'd dared dream. She continued a downward path until she kissed the smooth mounds that were the tops of Katie's breasts.

Her crotch spasmed at the feel of the silken cushions under her lips and against her cheeks. She brought her hand up and cupped the underside of Katie's breast through its satin confines.

Katie groaned in pleasure, and the sound brought Corrine to her senses. She abruptly sat up and tried to straighten her disheveled clothes.

"What's wrong? Why did you stop?"

"Katie…you're Della's daughter. This isn't right."

"I'm Katie Prentiss, the woman you've spent so much time with of late. You can't tell me you don't want this as badly as I do."

"Still, it's not right."

"It certainly felt right to me." Katie unbuttoned a button on Corrine's shirt. Then another.

Corrine grabbed her wrist. "We mustn't."

Katie wrestled her arm free and slipped her hand inside the open shirt. She lightly rubbed a hard nipple, and Corrine drew her breath.

"Katie, I implore you. I'm not this strong."

"Please don't be," she said before kissing Corrine again.

Corrine was dizzy with need as she gave herself over to Katie once again. She felt her mouth would surely be bruised from Katie's kisses. She didn't care. She kissed Katie with matched fervor as Katie's hand continued to tease her nipples.

She felt Katie's hand on her thigh, and her clit lurched just as the carriage came to a halt.

"Oh, damn!" Katie said. "Are we home already?"

"So it would seem." Corrine hastily buttoned her shirt and got her coat on just as the carriage door was opened for them.

Once inside the house, Katie was in Corrine's arms again. Corrine kissed her briefly but eventually pushed her away.

"It wouldn't do for your mother to come in and see us."

"She's asleep."

"We can't be sure of that."

"She'd be down here waiting for us if she was still awake."

Corrine held Katie close and stroked her soft hair. "I've very much enjoyed this evening. But it's time to say good night."

"You're almost as stubborn as I am."

Corrine laughed, took Katie's hand, and led her up the stairs.

"I'd rather be in your room than mine." Katie kissed her when they reached Corrine's room.

"Good night, Katie. I look forward to seeing you in the morning."

They kissed once more, and Corrine watched Katie walk to her room.

Alone in her room, Corrine slowly took off her clothes, reliving every moment of the night. She was craving more of Katie's kisses, even though she had just sent her away. She hung up her coat and vest. When she started unbuttoning her shirt, she could feel Katie's nimble fingers on them once again. Her skin was covered in gooseflesh by the time the shirt was off.

She held it to her nose and inhaled deeply of Katie's fresh scent. She laid the shirt on her bed and started at a knock on her door.

Expecting Della checking on their evening, she opened the door and saw Katie standing there in a dark blue satin robe. She walked in without waiting for an invitation.

"Katie, I don't think it wise that you're in here right now."

Katie said nothing. She stared into Corrine's eyes as she untied the sash on her robe.

Corrine's gaze fell to Katie's hands. She tried to say no, but nothing came out.

Katie slid her housecoat off and stood naked before Corrine.

Corrine couldn't breathe. She could barely tear her focus from the young, firm breasts laid bare for her. Her own cunt throbbed when she looked to the dark auburn patch where Katie's legs met.

Katie crossed the room and stood in front of Corrine. She took one of Corrine's hands and placed it on her breast, then kissed her.

Corrine closed her hand around the large mound and dragged her thumb across the hardening nipple poking at her. She kissed Katie with a passion she hadn't known she possessed. The kiss continued as Corrine walked Katie back to her bed. She laid her down then lay across her.

All thought was gone as she pressed her knee into Katie's wet center.

Katie moved her hands under Corrine's undershirt. She dragged her fingernails across Corrine's back. She brought them around to her chest and teasingly pinched her nipples.

Waves of heat rolled over Corrine. Her need was complete. Never had she wanted anyone like she wanted Katie Prentiss. She broke the kiss and looked deeply into Katie's eyes. The desire she saw reflected her own.

She swallowed hard and stood. "You should get dressed."

"What? You can't stop now."

"I must. This is Della's house. I can't do this."

Katie didn't move. She ran her hand down her body and spread her lower lips for Corrine. "You can't tell me you don't want this."

"I think you know better."

"Then take me. I'm offering myself to you."

Corrine picked Katie's housecoat from the floor and handed it to her. "Please. I'm fighting an internal battle here, but I must do what I know to be right. I'm begging you…if you care for me at all, you'll leave my room."

Katie slipped back into her robe. She opened the door to leave, but Corrine closed it and pressed her against it, kissing her with every ounce of pent-up passion burning inside her.

She pulled away and opened the door. "Good night, Katie."

"Good night."

Corrine closed the door behind Katie and leaned back against it. Every nerve in her body was on alert. She trembled as she stepped to the bed and lay there, fantasizing about all she and Katie could have done. She knew she was right in sending Katie back to her room, but even so, she knew she was fighting a losing battle. She didn't know how long she'd be able to deny that which they both so desperately wanted.

CHAPTER EIGHT

Katie sat restlessly as the priest droned on. She and her mother had left the house before Miss Staples was awake. She knelt while the other parishioners took communion and was thankful that Mass was almost over. She had butterflies in her stomach every time she thought of Miss Staples. Their night had been magical. She was a great kisser, and the thought of her hands on Katie made her blush. She felt like she should be angry or embarrassed because Miss Staples refused her when she lay there naked for her taking, but she believed Miss Staples was trying to do the right thing. It made her care even more deeply for her.

Mass was finally over and Katie and her mother were in the carriage back to the house.

"You're awfully quiet," her mother finally said.

"I'm sorry, Mama. I must just be tired."

"How was last night?"

Katie felt color creeping up her neck, and she turned away from her mother. "It was so much fun. I declare, I could spend every weekend like that."

Her mother laughed. "Well, don't get used to it, though I'm glad y'all had a good time. I expect to hear all about it over breakfast, as I'd imagine Cori will be awake when we arrive."

"Are you the only person who calls her Cori?"

"No. All her friends do. Or used to. I don't know any of her friends anymore."

Cori. Katie tried the name over her mind's tongue. It felt good. It felt right. It seemed so much more natural than Miss Staples. Still, before she called her Cori, she'd have to get used to calling her Corrine. Miss Staples seemed far too formal after the previous night.

"Certainly you're not thinking of addressing her in such a manner."

"Of course not," Katie lied. "I was simply asking."

The carriage pulled up in front of the house, and Katie had to stop herself from springing out and running up the stairs. It wouldn't do to make her mother suspicious, no matter how she longed to see and be with Corrine again.

They walked in to the aroma of bacon and eggs. Katie's stomach growled, but she cared more about finding Corrine than eating breakfast.

"I suppose I should go find Cori to see if she's breakfasted yet," her mother said.

"I'll get her." Katie half hoped she wouldn't find her downstairs so she could look in her room. Even though Corrine had turned her away the night before, just having her look at her naked body had taken her to new levels of arousal.

She found Corrine in the office. She walked in and wrapped her arms around her from behind. Corrine stiffened.

"Where is your mother?"

"Waiting on us for breakfast."

Corrine placed her hands on Katie's arms and leaned back into Katie's bosom. "I've been afraid I merely dreamed it and last night didn't happen."

"Kiss me?" Katie said

Corrine stood and took Katie in her arms. She hungrily devoured her lips, her tongue wasting no time entering Katie's mouth.

Katie's body was afire with the need one kiss created in her. The kiss ended quickly and Corrine held Katie close.

"What are we doing?" Corrine asked.

"We're adults. We're feeling what adults feel."

"My feelings are likely to get me in trouble. I fear I've little willpower where you're concerned."

"And I fear you have too much." Katie laughed.

They separated and each took a deep breath before wandering to the breakfast room, where they found Della sitting at a well-stocked table.

"This looks delicious," Corrine said.

"Where did you find her?" Della asked Katie.

"In the office."

"Cori, I appreciate your dedication and concern, but I must protest you working on a Sunday. That's not right."

"I'm determined to get to the bottom of the missing money."

"But I'm supposed to be working with you," Katie said. "And I won't work on a Sunday."

"Even if I find the problem today, I'll still instruct you on bookkeeping."

"And I'm afraid I must insist," Della said. "You've already done so much for us in the short time you've been here. Surely you'd enjoy a day to yourself?"

Corrine was conflicted. She would love a day off, but she'd been anticipating a day working side by side with Katie.

"Perhaps another day fishing would be good for you," Della said.

"That does sound nice." Corrine tried not to sound disappointed.

"I want to go fishing," Katie said.

"I must say, Katie, Miss Staples has been more than generous with her time. I think we should leave her alone for a day."

Corrine's heart leaped. She tried to sound impartial. "Of course, I'll not overstep whatever you deem appropriate for the girl, but I have no complaints about Katie fishing with me. Again, I'm not challenging your authority."

"I'll go have Maddy pack a picnic for us!"

With Katie out of the room, Della cast a hard gaze at Corrine. "I appreciate all you're doing for her. I hope you know that. But her behavior toward you is unsettling to me."

Corrine's stomach was in knots. Here it came. She didn't know if she'd be able to deny the accusation. She'd never lied to Della before. Della was the first person she'd told of her sexual proclivities as a teen. She felt horrible about her feelings for Katie but feared she'd admit to them if confronted. She searched for a fitting response but could only come up with, "I'm not certain I understand."

"As you know, I was very embarrassed about how rude and disrespectful she was less than a week ago. And now she wants to do everything you do. I feel she has no sense of propriety with you."

"Do you worry that I need to set clearer boundaries? I enjoy her company, so you need not worry about that."

"And I'm grateful for that. But I've never seen her behave this way. As I said, I find it unsettling."

"How so? Please speak what's on your mind."

"I've just never seen her act this way. I suppose I'm apologizing and making sure you're truly fine with it."

"I feel there's more."

"I don't know. Something seems off, and I hope she's not a burden to you."

"I assure you she's not. I find her to be an engaging young woman."

"Well, thank you then. For everything."

"It's my pleasure. Honestly." Her body still hummed with the tension. She'd have to talk to Katie and let her know she thought her mother was suspicious. "Now, if you'll excuse me, I'll go dress in my riding clothes and let Katie know I'm ready to leave."

Della took hold of Corrine's hand. "I love you, Cori. I honestly don't know what I'd do without you."

"We've been friends too long to ever worry about that." The words rang untrue in her ears.

❖

"I fear your mother has suspicions about us." Corrine said when she and Katie were preparing their horses for the ride.

"How could she?" Katie pressed herself into Corrine. Corrine backed into a wall, then felt trapped.

"She says your behavior unsettles her." Corrine willed herself to stay strong, even with Katie's body molded to hers.

"My behavior has always unsettled her." She tried to claim Corrine's lips, but Corrine turned her head, and Katie placed the kiss on her cheek.

Corrine placed her hands on Katie's shoulders and put some distance between them.

"Katie, I'm serious. I won't lose Della."

"But you would lose me?" Katie stepped back, pouting.

"I don't wish to lose you either."

"Well, you certainly make it sound like I'm something you can toss aside."

"That's not true. You must know that. But surely you can see my dilemma."

"I think you're making too much of it. Mother has no reason to be suspicious."

"Promise me you'll be careful around her. Please."

"Why don't we simply tell her about us?"

"Katie! This isn't a joking matter."

"Who's joking?"

Corrine closed the distance between them and looked into Katie's eyes, trying to determine whether she was serious.

"This isn't a game to me. I'm torn between my feelings for you and my friendship with your mother. Could you try to be understanding?"

"What are your feelings for me, exactly?" she said.

"Will you be serious for a moment?"

"Fine! I'll be more careful around Mother. Happy?"

"I wish I felt more confident that you mean that."

Katie's demeanor softened. "I mean it, Cori. I don't want to lose you. I'll be extra careful henceforth."

Corrine's heart skipped a beat. "What did you call me?"

"Was that wrong?"

Corrine looked around. Certain they were alone, she took Katie in her arms. "I like it so much better than Miss Staples. Say it again."

"Kiss me, Cori."

Corrine was happy to oblige. She softly brushed Katie's lips with her own. They were soft and pliant and opened immediately for her tongue. She slowly moved her tongue over and around Katie's, the tenderness of the kiss causing her passion to flare.

She ended the kiss and, breathless, held Katie to her.

Katie stepped out of her embrace and went back to preparing her horse for the fishing trip. "You never answered my question."

Corrine took her lead and placed a saddle on the bay. "What question is that, sweetheart?"

"What are your feelings for me?"

Corrine stared at Katie's back as she busied herself with her ebony horse. She longed to cup the shapely ass hugged in the fitted riding skirt she wore. She cleared her throat. "I'm falling in love with you."

Katie spun and faced her, her face alight with a brilliant smile. "Do you mean that?"

"I do."

Katie ran into her arms and hugged her tightly. "Oh, Cori, I'm falling in love with you, too. Isn't it wonderful?"

Corrine laughed at her exuberance. "Yes, it is. Now how about we get ready and get out of here?"

"Why don't you just ride with me? Spirit can carry both of us."

"You have a horse named Spirit?" She laughed. "How appropriate."

"You wouldn't have given me a second glance if I were a wallflower. Admit it."

"Correction. With the way you look, I would have given you a third and fourth glance, as well. But I doubt I would have fallen for you if you weren't so feisty."

"Feisty? I like that. So what do you say? Shall we ride together?"

Corrine let her imagination wander to her arms around Katie atop the horse, the feel of her breasts pressed into Katie's back as she bounced. She was getting wet again. She needed to get control of herself.

"Pleasant though I imagine that would be, I think it best that we take two horses. It would be hard to explain to your mother if she were to discover we only took one."

Katie sighed. "You worry an awful lot about things that likely will never happen. But I'll allow you may have a point. Let's finish getting ready then."

Corrine loaded the fishing gear into the special tackle bag and strapped it on the bay. Katie loaded the picnic supplies on Spirit. They rode side by side on the sunny fall day, the sweet scent of sugar cane in the air.

They rode past Corrine's previous fishing hole and came to a stop at a spot on the river that had a stand of oaks on the bank. Katie spread the blanket in the shade of the trees while Corrine baited the hooks and cast their lines. She propped them on broken branches and turned to see Katie lying on her back, using a saddlebag as a pillow.

Corrine moved to stand over her. "You certainly look comfortable."

Katie opened an eye. "I am, quite. Join me?"

Corrine lay on her side and propped herself up with her elbow as she gazed at Katie.

"That's an interesting cravat you've got on. It looks rather masculine."

"It was a tie of my father's"

"Katie! What would your mother say?"

"Not her again." Katie closed her eyes.

"I can't help it. She's my best friend. And you're wearing her dead husband's clothes."

"I also happen to be wearing my dead father's tie. Maybe I feel closer to him when I do."

"Oh, sweetheart. I'm so sorry. How heartless of me."

Katie opened her eyes again and stared at Corrine. "I hope you'll see what I mean. Your first thought is always my mother. I should think you'd worry about my feelings more."

"I shall try to be better. I promise."

"I'm sure I'll be able to forgive you. Especially when you use words like sweetheart with me."

"So you noticed?"

"I did. And I liked it."

"I'm glad."

Katie sat up. "So do you like my riding habit?"

"I like how anything looks on you."

"Did you like how nothing looked on me?"

"Very much."

Katie kissed Corrine, rolling her onto her back so she was on top of her. Corrine wrapped her arms around Katie and pressed her breasts against her chest. She couldn't get enough of the feel of Katie's young, supple body.

When the kiss ended, Katie rolled onto her back again, and Corrine lay on her side. She lazily dragged her hand between Katie's breasts.

"Katie, I have to ask you a personal question."

"After last night, I'd think you'd know I have nothing to hide."

The mention of her nudity the night before set Corrine's body on fire. "I enjoyed the sight of you with nothing to hide."

"What's your question?"

"Have you ever made love?"

"What do you think?"

"I don't know what to think. After last night, I'd have to guess I won't be your first."

"Does that sadden you?"

"I'm conflicted. I would like to think you're untouched, but the way you seemed to know what you were doing was quite arousing."

"I'm glad I arouse you."

"That you do. So I'm correct that you're not inexperienced?"

"You are correct."

"Have you ever been with a woman?" Corrine was tense awaiting the answer, not sure which answer she wanted to hear.

"Would you rather I have or not?"

"I'd rather an honest answer."

Katie propped herself up and looked directly into Corrine's eyes. "I've only been with women."

"Women? So there have been many?"

"Not many. Two. But neither was serious. They were for fun and experimenting."

"Am I an experiment? An older, more experienced woman?"

"So you are quite experienced? I wondered." She smiled.

"You didn't answer my question."

"No, you're not an experiment."

Corrine leaned forward and took Katie's mouth with hers. Her kiss started softly, tenderly, but soon she was light-headed with desire, and her kiss intensified.

Katie lay back down, and they continued to kiss as Corrine closed her hand over one of Katie's breasts. Katie moaned in her mouth, and Corrine pressed into her, wrapping a leg over hers to feel pressure against her sensitive clit. She lightly thrust against her as she unbuttoned Katie's shirt.

Katie slid her hand between her hip and Corrine, but Corrine pulled away.

"What?" Katie asked.

"Not so fast, love. We've all day. I don't want to hurry this."

She kissed her again and slipped her hand under the shirt to feel Katie's free breasts. She broke the kiss and pulled Katie to a sitting position. Together they got Katie's shirt over her head.

Corrine stared lovingly at the soft mounds exposed for her. She lowered her mouth to one and sucked deeply on the pink nipple. Her tongue rolled over and under it, teasing it harder. She moved to the other exposed nipple and took the first between her finger and thumb. Aware of every movement, Corrine made certain to be more tender than she normally would be. Her encounters with nameless women tended to get rough, but she didn't want that with Katie. This would be special.

She twisted the nipple as she sucked and licked the other. She moved her hand lower, over the slight swell of Katie's stomach, and behind her to cup her ass. She squeezed it harder than she'd intended, but Katie arched into her.

"I've wanted to do this since last week in the stables."

"I wanted you to do this then."

"Your ass is shaped so fine. It's made for me to grab and squeeze."

"I get aroused when you talk like that."

"Katie," she whispered hoarsely, "I want always to have my hand on your soft ass so I may squeeze it whenever I want."

"It makes me wet when you say that."

Corrine's cunt throbbed. "I want to make you wetter than anyone ever has."

Katie grabbed Corrine's hand and pressed it between her legs. "Can you feel me?"

"I can." She wanted to place her hand inside Katie right then but was determined to make it last. She moved her hand back to her ass and went back to kneading it as she kissed her hard on the mouth again.

Katie quickly unbuttoned Corrine's shirt and pulled it over her head. She moved both hands to fondle her small breasts. Corrine gasped as Katie played with them. Her body was alive with need, the need to feast on Katie's body and to have Katie feast on hers. She wanted to please and be pleased. She was certain the exchange of pleasure between them would surpass anything she'd ever experienced.

When Katie took a breast in her mouth, Corrine grabbed her head and held it in place. Her eyes closed with passion. Her free hand trembling, she fumbled with the buttons on Katie's skirt.

Katie helped slide it off and straddled Corrine's belly while she kissed her on her mouth.

"You feel so good. You're so wet. Keep rubbing against me," Corrine said when Katie moved her mouth to her neck to suck.

Katie reached behind her and tried to unbutton Corrine's britches. "I've got them." Corrine quickly finished undressing while Katie slid down her body to suck her breasts.

Corrine rolled Katie onto her back and suckled her nipples more while she moved her hand along her inner thighs. She dragged it from her knee slowly up her thigh until she felt Katie's hair on the back of her hand. Then she dragged it back down.

Katie was writhing below her, arching her hips. "Please touch me."

"Not yet."

"I can't take much more."

"You might be surprised."

Corrine kissed Katie on the mouth again, then flipped her over so Katie was on her belly. Her breasts pressed into Katie's back and her hard clit poked against her ass. She kissed the back of her neck as she ground into her.

She kissed down her back and finally kissed and licked her soft, firm cheeks while she continued to squeeze them.

Katie arched her back and watched Corrine. "I've heard stories of what you're going to do."

"Hmm?" Corrine asked distractedly.

"No one's ever, I mean, I've never. Nobody's been in there before."

Corrine came to her senses and rested her cheek on a fleshy buttock. "Oh, sweetheart, I'm not going to do that. Has anyone ever entered you from behind?"

"I just said—"

"No, not there. Climb on your hands and knees for me."

Corrine went back to kissing the tight ass and kneaded Katie's inner thigh. She slowly moved her hand up and finally rubbed it against Katie's dripping cunt.

"Oh, sweetheart. You are so ready for me." She slipped two fingers inside.

"You feel so deep."

"Mm-hmm. You're so tight, baby. You feel so good." She continued moving in and out and added another finger, which slid easily into the slickness.

She held back, fighting the urge to slip her whole hand inside. She knew she needed to change positions before she lost control. She removed her fingers and helped Katie lay on her back again.

"Why did you stop?"

"Relax." She kissed Katie's mouth, her neck, and luscious breasts. She kissed down her belly until she was kneeling between her legs.

She paused for a moment and gazed at the swollen wet lips and engorged clitoris.

"You're so beautiful." She bent and licked every inch of Katie, from the tip of her clit to her cunt, which was begging for her. She buried her tongue inside and licked the satin walls, lapping at the juices that were flowing there.

"Oh, God, yes. That's it." Katie tangled her fingers in Corrine's hair and held tight while she moved against her mouth. She bucked and moved around, coating Corrine's face.

Corrine held tight to Katie's ass and followed her lead, licking as deeply as she could, then moving her tongue to flick her clit. She finally settled her mouth on her clit, sucking and licking while she slipped her fingers inside again. With her free hand, she pinched and teased a nipple. She was connected to Katie in every possible way. She wanted more, craved more, wanted to climb all the way inside her.

She was lost in her lovemaking, surrounded by Katie, and there she wanted to stay. She continued to love her clit and cunt, pressing deeper and licking harder until Katie stopped her bucking and held Corrine's face in place. She kept sucking and licking as Katie screamed, her whole body trembling, her cunt seizing Corrine's fingers and pulling them deeper.

"That was amazing," Katie said when she could find her breath.

"It certainly was." Corrine continued to softly lick and kiss her.

Katie tugged gently on her hair. "Come kiss me. I want to taste that."

Corrine arched an eyebrow and smiled. "My pleasure." She leaned her body into Katie and kissed her mouth hard, slipping her tongue inside. Their kiss was frantic, their passion far from satiated.

"That was delicious."

"I have to agree." Corrine took Katie in her arms.

"I'm afraid I'm a puddle at the moment." Katie backed into Corrine.

"That's very nice to hear."

"But what about you?" Katie said sleepily.

"You won't be a puddle all day," Corrine whispered, then closed her eyes as well.

CHAPTER NINE

Corrine woke to pleasant sensations coursing through her body. Fully awake, she realized they stemmed from Katie's mouth on her nipple.

"So you're awake?" she asked.

Katie opened her eyes and smiled, her teeth still on a nipple. "I like the way you woke me."

Katie released her hold and moved to lie on top of Corrine. "I couldn't stand the sight of your naked body going unpleasured."

"I appreciate that."

Katie put her hand between Corrine's legs. "You're wet."

Corrine took her hand away and placed it in Katie's mouth. "I was dreaming of you."

"Your flavor is unbelievable." She kissed Corrine's mouth and shared.

"I love your kisses," Corrine said when they finally broke for air.

Katie moved her hand down to Corrine's cleft while she resumed sucking a nipple.

Corrine lay back and closed her eyes as the feelings washed over her. Her nipple ached from Katie's bites. The sensation sent heat surging to the nerve center Katie was stroking. She wanted to stop Katie and take over. She wanted to fuck Katie hard and fast.

Her body made her crazy, but she forced herself to relax and let Katie please her. She knew it was what Katie wanted.

Her stomach rippled as Katie trailed kisses down it. She moaned at the feel of Katie's wet cunt sliding over her leg. Katie pressed her center onto Corrine's leg as she licked circles around Corrine's hardened clit. Corrine throbbed at Katie's attention. She smiled at Katie's teasing, knowing she could outlast her. Her breath caught when Katie closed her teeth around her clit and sucked hard, flicking the sensitive tip with her tongue.

She looked down and got even wetter at the sight of Katie's auburn hair fanned across her legs as she continued to suck and bite. She placed her hand on the back of Katie's head and pressed her harder into her center.

Katie teased Corrine's cunt by lightly dragging her fingers around her opening and squeezing her wet, swollen lips. She finally slid a finger inside and probed deeply while she lapped at her clit.

"Darlin', I need more than that," Corrine said.

Katie slipped one, then two more fingers inside and gently stroked Corrine's inner walls.

Corrine smiled at her soft touch. Tender or not, the idea that it was Katie inside her helped lead her to the edge of reality. She closed her eyes and focused all her attention on the responses her body was having to Katie's ministrations. Her clit was about to burst as Katie licked it.

"Put your teeth on me again. Please…"

Katie sucked her clit between her teeth once more, and it took only one more flick of her tongue for Corrine to feel her body tense in anticipation. The orgasm racked her body, and she rode the pleasure for what seemed an eternity. The spasms finally ceased, and she helped Katie into her arms.

Katie lay staring into Corrine's eyes.

"What is it, love?"

"Just admiring you."

"You look like you have something on your mind."

"Did I do everything in a pleasing manner?"

"What? Katie Prentiss is having a moment of insecurity?" Corrine laughed.

Katie sat up, crossed her legs, and folded her arms over her chest. "I'm not sure I enjoy being laughed at."

Corrine reached out and unfolded her arms. "Never hide those from me, lover."

"I like it when you look at me."

"I like to look at you." She leaned forward and sucked briefly on a tit. "I like to suck you."

She let her gaze fall to Katie's exposed cunt. "Do you like when I look at you there?"

"Very much." Katie reached between her legs and spread her lips for Corrine. "Do you like what you see?"

"Very much."

Corrine kissed her hard on her mouth.

Katie pulled away. "You have a bad habit of not answering my questions."

"Forgive me," Corrine said, her gaze on her hand caressing Katie's breast. "What was the question again?"

"You're so experienced. I fear I didn't please you as well as I should."

"Sweetheart, please. Everything you do pleases me."

"I'm not convinced."

"I mean it. The sight of you arouses me. Your touch sets me on fire. You please me very much."

"But you had to tell me what to do a couple of times."

"It's all part of learning. We'll learn each other's likes and dislikes. It was our first time together. And it was wonderful."

"Did you enjoy making love to me?"

"Dear God, woman! Have you seen your body? It was made for me to pleasure."

"I felt like you were holding back. I may not be as experienced as you, but I'm not a fragile vessel, either."

"When I make love to you, I'm not thinking, I'm only doing. And I do wish you'd stop referring to my experience. It only serves to remind me how much older I am than you. And I assure you, that's not arousing."

"I find your age and experience very arousing. I just want to be sure you know that you needn't treat me like a delicate flower."

Corrine tried not to let her enjoyment of that comment show. "I appreciate that."

Katie lay back, spread her legs, and began stroking her clitoris. "I didn't mean to ruin the mood."

"Oh, the mood's coming back." Corrine watched Katie's hand lightly rubbing her enlarging clit. "Please don't stop."

Katie bent her knees and let them fall open so Corrine could see her better. "I told you I like it when you look at me."

"You're a sensual woman, Katie Prentiss."

"Will you touch yourself for me?"

"I don't know about that."

Katie closed her legs.

"No! Don't do that. Okay, okay." Corrine ran her fingers along her cunt and felt her body tingle as she looked at Katie and saw the desire in her eyes. She was happy that Katie didn't mind stepping over some lines.

"I'd rather be touching you." Corrine lay on top of Katie and kissed her mouth. Their tongues rolled over each other, fueled by frantic need. Gone was the exploratory caution of earlier. They kissed with reckless abandon as Corrine brought her knee up against Katie.

Katie traced her nipples, leaving a trail of her juices for Corrine to enjoy, which she did as she moved her mouth to the tits and licked every drop off them.

She kissed Katie again and twisted her nipples. First one and then the other, she pinched and twisted. Katie responded by wrapping her legs around Corrine's. She rubbed against her as their kiss grew more passionate. The feel and taste of Katie made Corrine lose all reason. She quit thinking and let her desires take over.

She pulled her leg away from Katie and drove her fingers inside her. Three fingers in deep, then slowly pulled back out, then back in as deep as they could go. Katie spread her legs wider.

"Yes! Oh, God, that feels wonderful!"

Corrine pulled her hand out and rolled Katie over. She grabbed her under her waist and pulled her back so Katie's ass was pressed against her breasts. She held her there and plunged four fingers in her cunt. She twisted her hand and pulled it back out. Again, she pushed them in. Katie was so tight. The feel of her walls pressing against her drove her on, and she fucked her harder with each thrust.

Katie was dripping, her juices flowing down Corrine's hand, as she continued to drill her from behind.

"You like that?"

"Oh, yes! Fuck me, Cori. I've never felt so full!"

Corrine bit her ass as she fucked her, getting hotter by the minute as Katie wriggled on her hand. She moved her free hand to Katie's clit and rubbed furiously.

Katie screamed as she came, her cunt constricting over and over around Corrine's hand, inflicting sweet pain on her.

When the spasms subsided, Corrine rolled Katie over onto her back and knelt between her knees, throwing her legs over her shoulders. She moved her tongue in a frenzy over Katie's sensitive clit. She slid her fingers back inside and filled her hard and fast. She closed her lips around her swollen morsel and sucked as hard as she could.

Katie was bucking against her. Corrine glanced up and saw Katie's head thrashing. She reached to pinch a nipple while she sucked and fucked her. She lapped at her clit again, pressing her tongue into her as hard as she could. She felt her cunt twitch and then contract on her hand.

She didn't wait until Katie's breathing returned to normal before she moved to her breast and sucked her nipple through her teeth. She pulled her hand out of her and rubbed her clit. She pressed it against Katie's pubis, loving the feel of it trapped between two hard forces.

"I can't," Katie protested.

"Oh, yes, you can." Corrine attacked the other nipple with her mouth.

Katie was spent. She had never come so hard and never one right after the other like that. Her clit was sore, and she was surprised it hadn't receded to the safety of its hood. Yet, as Corrine rubbed her sensitive shaft, she felt the now familiar prickling sensation that began at the center of her being and worked its way out until she exploded, the orgasms racking her body. White heat shot through her until she was finally able to think clearly.

She lay exhausted and almost afraid that Corrine would take her one more time.

"I'll never move again," she said.

"You don't have to move anything but your tongue," Corrine said as she lowered herself onto Katie's mouth.

Katie felt her body coming alive as she licked at Corrine's turgid clit. Corrine was wet and slick and tasted salty and musky. Katie was becoming aroused again as Corrine moved on her face. Up and down and back and forth she moved, and Katie tried to follow her lead. Corrine was fucking her face and Katie was enjoying another first. She grasped Corrine's ass and guided her over her tongue.

Corrine gasped at the feel of Katie moving her as her tongue worked her. She was more aroused than she'd ever been, and she knew it would take no time at all to come on Katie's face. She looked down and saw Katie's face buried beneath her twat, and the sight combined with Katie's actions took her over the edge. Katie's tongue hit just the right spot at just the right moment and sent Corrine sailing. She came hard, one orgasm after another as Katie kept her tongue moving until Corrine was depleted. She climbed off Katie and lay next to her, pulling her close again.

"Your tongue is like magic, sweetheart. That was unbelievable."

They lay in each other's arms. Corrine was getting restless again and kissed Katie softly on the neck. She sucked an earlobe and finally claimed her mouth. Katie kissed back with a vengeance.

Corrine skimmed her hand over Katie's body. She brushed over her nipples, rubbing her palms over them and smiling as they poked her. Moving lower, she teased the curls where Katie's legs met. Katie held Corrine's mouth to hers as she opened her legs.

"I love how ready you always are," Corrine murmured against Katie's lips as she guided her hand down to Katie's folds. She delicately moved her fingers over her wet clit, urging it out to play.

"And I love what you do to me."

Katie's body responded yet again. Corrine was gentle. She ran her fingers along Katie's cunt, before slowly slipping one inside. She traced her walls and then pulled her finger out.

"Are you okay?" Corrine asked.

Katie nodded.

Corrine teased a nipple with her tongue, still playing nice, and Katie let out a low moan. She put two fingers in Katie, who spread her legs wider. Corrine separated her fingers as she pulled them out and dragged them over Katie's clit, now fully at attention. She moved them back inside and kissed her way down Katie's belly.

She lightly licked at Katie's clit while she pulled her fingers out and reinserted them. She twisted her hand inside her while she loved her with her mouth. She felt Katie's hand lying softly on her hair and was happy that she was able to take her again.

She continued to lick and play with her clit while her fingers moved in and out. She took her time and slowly but deliberately gave Katie another climax.

"I love your body, Katie Prentiss."

"And it loves you." She smiled.

CHAPTER TEN

With the afternoon almost gone, Corrine watched sadly as Katie covered her luscious body with clothing. "I wish you could always be naked."

"I'd like to always be naked for you, for you to take whenever you desire."

"We'd never get anything done, I'm afraid."

"We could hire a competent staff and never worry about anything but loving each other."

"I do like the sound of that." Corrine stood and began getting dressed.

"I'm famished," Katie said.

"We didn't touch the picnic." Corrine laughed.

"What shall we do with it? It will look suspicious for us to show up at the house with it."

Corrine grabbed some of the food and walked to the riverbank. She tossed the food in, then began reeling in the fishing lines.

"Our bait is gone. I suppose we may have gotten some nibbles."

"I was enjoying the nibbles I was getting." Katie smiled.

They dumped the rest of the food into the water and packed up their picnic site.

Katie looked around. "There's nothing left here of our lovemaking."

"There is here, though." Corrine rubbed Katie between her legs.

"Mmm. There will be for a long time."

Corrine grabbed Katie and kissed her one last time before they mounted the horses.

"Oh my, this is a little painful." Katie adjusted herself in the saddle.

"Just wait until tomorrow." Corrine laughed.

They took their time on the ride back to the house, mostly in deference to Katie's soreness. Still, the house came into view far too soon, signaling that their special day had come to an end.

They saw to their horses, then were in each other's arms once again in the stables, mouths pressed together, tongues dancing over each other. When they finally ended the kiss, they held each other, breathless.

"Come on then, we'd better get in the house."

"I don't want to," Katie said.

"We have no choice. Now remember, we mustn't do anything to raise suspicions."

"So I can't sit on your lap during dinner?"

"Katie, I'm serious."

"You're too serious. But I don't wish to fight after the day we had. I promise to behave."

Della was waiting on the porch as they walked up. "I saw you ride up. So will we be having fish for dinner?"

Corrine's stomach knotted. "I'm afraid we had no luck with the fish today."

"Well, you both look relaxed, so I'll assume the day was pleasant."

"It was wonderful, Mama." Katie kissed Della's cheek, and Corrine's heart skipped a beat. She was sure her fragrance would be lingering on Katie's face, and she didn't like her that close to her mother.

"I'm happy to hear that."

"If you'll excuse me," Corrine said, "I must wash up before dinner."

Della looked at Katie. "And you'll be wanting to change for dinner, I'm sure."

"I most certainly will." Katie hurried into the house after Corrine. She followed her up the stairs and leaned against her when they got to Corrine's room.

"We need to be careful. Your mother is right downstairs," Corrine whispered.

"And we're upstairs." Katie sought Corrine's mouth.

"Please don't do this."

Katie reached around Corrine and opened her door. She pushed her into the room and closed the door behind them. "Now?"

Against her better judgment, Corrine gave in and was soon lost in the kiss. She grabbed Katie's ass and pulled her against her, grinding her pelvis into her. Desire flared and all she wanted to do was throw Katie on the bed and take her once again.

She came to her senses and finally took her mouth off Katie's. "We must be more careful," she said.

"No one can see us in here."

"Your mother is waiting supper on us. We need to dress for dinner. I'll see you downstairs."

"Fine." Katie twitched her ass for Corrine as she walked out of her room.

❖

Corrine scrubbed her face and hands before she selected her clothes for dinner. Satisfied that Katie's scent no longer covered her, she dressed in gray trousers, a red vest, and black coat. She went downstairs to find Della waiting in the living room.

"Why, don't you look fetching?"

"Thank you, kind lady. You look quite radiant yourself." She thought Della was very attractive, even in the basic black she always wore. "I would think you'll be looking forward to wearing color again soon."

"I feel as though I could wear black forever. I don't know that I'll ever feel right gaily dressed."

"Oh, Della." Corrine took her in her arms. "Time will heal your wound."

Corrine saw movement out of the corner of her eye and looked up to see Katie on the landing. Katie's eyes hardened at the sight of Della in Corrine's arms.

"Am I interrupting something?" Katie descended the stairs.

Della stepped out of Corrine's arms and wiped her eyes. "I've just been missing your father so much lately."

"Oh, Mama, I'm so sorry." Katie hugged her mother but kept her cold gaze on Corrine. Corrine hated the cool glare and wondered if Katie was angry, thinking she'd made Della cry again.

Della led the way to the dining room. Corrine grabbed Katie's arm and spoke softly. "So you're upset because I made your mother cry? I didn't this time."

"No. I don't like spending a day making love with you, and the minute I'm out of the room, you have my mother in your arms."

"She was upset!"

"I suppose any excuse will do."

"Surely you're not jealous."

Katie stormed after Della, leaving Corrine dumbfounded.

❖

At dinner, Katie and Corrine rapidly devoured their food, having not eaten all day.

"You two act like you're starving. Didn't you take a picnic with you?"

Corrine glanced at Katie. "We took a picnic. It must be all that fresh air and exercise."

Corrine choked on a mouthful of yams.

"Exercise?" Della asked. "There must be more to fishing than I realized. When I'd go with your father, he'd throw the line out, then relax in the sun while I did needlepoint. That hardly built up an appetite."

"We walked up and down the shore quite a bit," Corrine lied.

"Whatever you did, you both look happy, and there's nothing wrong with a healthy appetite."

Corrine felt the color rising to her cheeks, so she stared at her plate.

"I definitely feel more alive," Katie said.

"What else did you do besides walk around?"

Corrine and Katie looked at each other, but neither spoke for a few minutes.

"I know I fell asleep at least once," Katie offered.

Corrine could think of nothing to say, so she remained silent as she finished her dinner.

When dessert was over, Katie excused herself and beat a hasty retreat upstairs.

Corrine joined Della on the porch.

"Have you told me everything that happened today?" Della asked.

Corrine's heart stopped briefly. "Whatever do you mean?"

"Something seemed off with you two this evening. Are you sure she wasn't insolent or discourteous?"

"I assure you, it was a very pleasant day."

"You know, Cori, I trust you."

Guilt washed over her. "I should hope so."

"So I expect you to tell me when something's not right. I can't be having you taking Katie's side, you understand."

Corrine felt caught between a rock and a hard place. Both women meant the world to her, but she felt as though no matter whom she spent time with or talked to, she was betraying the other. She questioned if there was any way for her to come out of the situation unscathed.

"You have my word that if she and I have any issues or if she gives me any problems, I'll be sure to inform you. But please know nothing like that happened today."

"I believe you. Still, something wasn't quite right tonight. Or maybe that was simply the imagination of a lonely old woman."

"Della, please. I'm sorry you're so lonely, but you are far from old. After all," she said, "we're the same age."

"I know, but I feel old of late. Quite frankly, I'm afraid to go back to society. I fear I'll become a hermit or some such."

"That won't happen as long as I'm around. Once your period of mourning is up, I'll take both of you to the opera."

"I do appreciate that, Cori. You know how I love the opera. I'm just not certain I'll ever be able to enjoy it again."

"It'll take some time, but you need to do it. It won't do for you to cut yourself off from everyone forever."

"I know what you're saying is true, but I still don't feel like I want to put forth the effort."

"No need to worry about that until the time gets here, at any rate."

"You are so right. If you'll excuse me, I'm going to turn in for the night."

"I'll be doing that soon. First, I'm going to have a cigar and enjoy the pleasant evening."

"Good night then."

❖

Left alone with her thoughts, Corrine questioned what she was doing with Katie. She could be making a giant mistake. Be that as it may, she knew she couldn't walk away from her. Katie had a definite hold on her, much more so after partaking of her body all day.

She was smoking a cigar and lost in her thoughts when she heard the front door close. Katie joined her on the porch wearing her housecoat over her nightgown. She walked over and leaned over Corrine, her breasts brushing lightly against her chest as she kissed her.

"That was nice," Corrine said. "Not safe, but nice. I thought you had retired for the night."

"I was simply giving you and my mother time alone. You seem to need that."

"Honestly, what's that supposed to mean?"

"It's quite obvious that you're fine alone with me. And alone with her. But when you're with both of us, you get quite uncomfortable. I can't help but wonder why."

"My best friend happens to be my lover's mother. I can't imagine why I'm uncomfortable either." Sarcasm dripped from every word.

"Do you think of her as my mother?"

"What do you mean?"

"Do you think of me as her daughter?"

"Stop with the word games, I implore you. Be up front with your thoughts."

"Today. Did you fuck me? Or Della's daughter?"

"Katie! Keep your voice down. My Lord. No, she didn't cross my mind while we were making love."

"When you talk to her, is she my mother or Della?"

Corrine thought for a moment. "She's both. What are you getting at?"

Katie just smiled, then hugged Corrine. "That makes me happy."

"I'm afraid you've lost me."

"Don't you see? When you're alone with me like that, you don't think of her."

"Of course not."

"But when you're alone with her, you still think of me."

"True. But I'm never alone with her 'like that.'"

"I think I believe you now."

"How could you ever think such a thing about your mother?"

"I've seen the way you look at her."

"I assure you, I've *never* had those feelings for her. Ever."

"Maybe you've just never admitted it to yourself. My concern was that you thought of her while you were inside me. I believe now that you didn't."

"Did I not make my feelings for you clear?"

"You did. That doesn't make your feelings for her clear. This conversation is starting to bore me. I believe you are more in love with me than you are her, so I'm happy. Shall we go to bed?"

"Not together, Katie," Corrine said.

"I know. But we can go upstairs together."

"That we can." She extinguished her cigar and stood, offering her hand to Katie, who took it and stood as well. She held Corrine's hand longer than necessary, and they stared into each other's eyes. Desire smoldered between them. Corrine knew how easy it would be to bed Katie right then. She was grateful Katie didn't realize that.

They walked up the stairs together and stopped in the hall outside Corrine's room.

"Aren't you going to invite me in?"

"I don't think that would be wise."

"You think too much."

Common sense warred with lust as Corrine stared at Katie's figure barely concealed from her. What harm would there be in a kiss or two?

She opened the door and allowed Katie to enter first. She closed and locked the door behind them. Taking Katie's hand, she led her to the bed. Katie sat and Corrine joined her. She brushed a stray hair off Katie's face and kept her hand on her soft hair.

"You are so very beautiful," Corrine whispered. "I swear, your beauty takes my breath away."

"I like that I have that effect on you."

Corrine lightly brushed her lips against Katie's. "Do you know how hard it is for me to keep my hands off you?"

"I wish you never would." She placed her hands on Corrine's face and drew her back to her. She kissed Corrine with the passion of a new lover. Her lips pressed hard into Corrine's, her tongue moving along Corrine's lips, begging for access to her mouth.

Corrine parted her lips and welcomed Katie's tongue. Her breath caught at the feel of their tongues moving over each other. She pulled away for air. "Dear God, Katie. What you do to me."

She laid Katie on the bed and lay next to her, kissing her voraciously as she deftly untied the sash on Katie's housecoat. She slid her hand under the silky material and dragged it over her breasts, which were covered only by the thin material of her nightgown. Corrine bent to suck a nipple through the gown and was rewarded with Katie's hands on her head, holding her in place.

She licked at the hardened nipple, coaxing it harder. She cupped the full breast, then moved to pinch the nipple while her mouth moved to the other one.

Her body alive with passion, she pressed herself against Katie, rocking into her.

Katie began unbuttoning Corrine's trousers, her fingers unsteady but determined. Corrine felt Katie's hand in her curls and grabbed her wrist. "Oh, no, you don't."

"But I want to feel you, to be in you. Please don't deny me."

Corrine rolled away. "I'm sorry. I got carried away. You have a way of making me take leave of my senses. But we mustn't go any further. Not tonight."

"You're teasing me, Cori. That's not nice."

"I didn't mean to. As I said, I got carried away. Please forgive me." She stood. "Now get yourself together and go to your room before my resolve weakens."

Katie stood and wrapped her arms around Corrine, resting her lips against hers. "But what if I want your resolve to weaken?"

Corrine removed her arms and stepped back. "As much as I appreciate that, I really must insist."

"Fine." Katie pouted. "But when will we make love again?"

"I don't know the answer to that, my love, but I assure you, I'll figure something out."

"Please do."

CHAPTER ELEVEN

Corrine walked into the office Monday morning to find Katie already dressed and hard at work.

"You're up early," she said.

"There's work to be done."

"Did you have breakfast?"

"No. Perhaps we can eat together after a bit?"

"That would be nice."

"How are you feeling this morning, down there?"

Katie laughed. "I'm quite sore, but I love the memories the pain evokes."

Corrine sat in her chair and looked at Katie, only inches from her.

"You look absolutely breathtaking," she whispered.

"Is it your intention to keep me wet?"

"Don't say those kinds of things to me."

"Well, you say the sweetest things. You make me want you."

"Now who's being a tease?"

"If I were being a tease, I'd do this." She pulled down her neckline and exposed a breast.

Corrine looked toward the door. "Katie! You can't be doing that. What if your mother had walked in?"

"But she didn't." Katie took Corrine's hand and placed it on her exposed flesh.

Corrine closed her eyes at the feel of the soft skin under her fingertips. She quickly regained her composure.

"Please put yourself together. It wouldn't do for Della to see your breast."

Katie tucked her breast away and turned back to the books. Corrine stared at her and wondered at her ability to focus so easily. She knew she needed to get to work but found it harder than ever to get her attention on the numbers she needed to review. The proximity of Katie made her head spin and her twat clench.

They worked in silence side by side. Corrine was finally absorbed in her work when she felt Katie's fingers moving steadily up her inner thigh. She jumped. "What are you doing?"

"Making sure you haven't forgotten me."

"That will never happen."

Katie looked toward the door while she stroked Corrine's crotch.

"Stop it!" Corrine said louder than she'd intended. Her outburst brought Della to the doorway.

"Is everything all right in here?"

"Everything is fine, Della. I didn't mean to raise my voice. I think it's a good time to take a break. Have you had breakfast?"

"I have, but there's plenty left. Just go ask Maddy. If you're certain everything is fine, I'll go back to the day room."

"We'll see you in a bit then," Corrine said. She looked at Katie. "I'll be eating if you need me."

Corrine found Maddy in the kitchen, helping a beautiful redhead at the stove. "Excuse me?"

The women turned and Corrine couldn't stop staring at the redhead. She was stunning, with hair on fire and eyes the color of the sea.

"Is there something you're needing?" the redhead asked with a thick brogue.

"I was hoping you might have some breakfast food left over."

"Go sit at the table, and Maddy here will bring you something."

"I'll be out in the breakfast nook."

"Fine."

Corrine turned to leave and bumped into Katie.

"Well, hello, Miss Katie," the redhead said. "How have you been?"

"Hello, Abigail," Katie said. "I'll be joining Miss Corrine for breakfast."

"I'll see to it Maddy is right out with food for the two of you."

They left the kitchen. "Miss Corrine?" Corrine asked.

"Miss Staples seems too formal."

"I concur, but should we not run that past your mother first?"

"I swear." Katie sighed. "I'd think you'd be able to decide what you'd like to be called without asking her permission."

"I'd rather Cori, and you damn well know it," Corrine said as they sat down.

"That simply won't do for my fragile mother, will it?"

"Why must you be this way? I swear, you exasperate me."

"I think we should tell my mother."

"And I think you've lost your mind."

"Why? Are you ashamed?"

"Katie, please. I have my reasons. I beg you to respect them."

"What about my wishes? Don't they count for anything?"

"Of course they do. I simply request we wait before we say something to Della."

"If we said something, we could be open, and I could hold your hand and kiss you when I want, and you could hold me at night because we could sleep together."

"What you describe sounds heavenly. I do hope in time things will be like that."

"I understand what you're saying, Cori. It's just that I want so badly—"

They grew silent as Maddy brought their food. Della walked in behind her.

"How are things now? Better?" she asked.

Neither was quick to respond.

"Everything is fine." It sounded like a lie even to Corrine's own ears.

"I feel tension, and I'd appreciate it if someone would tell me what's going on."

"There's no tension, Mama. It's simply the stress of looking over the books, trying to find when the money started disappearing."

"I hope that's all it is. I caution you again, Katie. If you are in any way an inconvenience to Cori, then your lessons cease."

"She's fine, Della. I fear I've been less than patient with her. I'll try to do better."

"You're here to help us. She shouldn't be underfoot. If she's not helping, she need not be in the office."

"I promise she's more of a help than a hindrance."

They were interrupted when Pierre came in to tell Della she had a visitor. When she was gone, Corrine said softly, "You know how I feel about you, Katie. That should be enough for you for now."

"I apologize for being such a brat. It is enough. It's just that you spoiled me so yesterday, and I want every day to be like that."

"If we solve the mystery of the missing money, we'll have more time like that."

Katie stared into Corrine's eyes, seeing the need that matched her own. "Fine. I'll try to behave."

"Now that that's settled, tell me, who was that woman in the kitchen with Maddy?"

"That was Abigail."

"So your mother has an Irish woman in charge of the kitchen."

"Yes. She runs the kitchen, her husband, Paddy, runs the stables, and their daughter, Mollie, cleans the house."

"Paddy? The one who was working the books?"

"The very one."

"I see."

"Shall we get back to work?"

Corrine kept her focus on the door as she reached out and cupped Katie's jaw. She lightly ran her thumb over her soft skin.

"I want you." Her voice was husky with need.

"I want to be naked for you again."

"Soon."

"When?"

"I don't know, but it must be soon."

Corrine and Katie went back to work and passed the afternoon in a comfortable silence; the only tension between them was sexual.

"You two have been awfully quiet." Della entered the office. "I would think you'd be hungry by now."

"What time is it?" Corrine asked.

"It's time for everyone to change for dinner. We have thirty minutes."

Corrine closed the ledger she was looking at and took Katie's from her. "Come on. Let's go change." To Della she said, "We'll be right down."

She and Katie went upstairs, and when they got to Corrine's door, she opened it and pulled Katie inside. She pressed her against the door and crushed her mouth with hers. Their kiss was hot and fast; all the pent up desire from the day together came out in the kiss.

Katie took Corrine's hand and led her to the bed.

"Katie, love, we really haven't the time for this."

Katie lay down and hiked her dress up, exposing her naked twat for Corrine, who gazed lovingly at it. She reached down and traced Katie's cleft before pushing a fingertip inside her. The slick heat fueled her fire. She took her finger out and put it in Katie's mouth to suck.

Katie ran her tongue over Corrine's finger as she greedily sucked it deeper. When she released her grip on it, Corrine kissed her and traced her cunt with her hand. She finally broke the kiss and stood.

"Are you always in the habit of not wearing pantalettes?"

"I told you I like when you look at me. I was hoping to have your eyes on me today."

"You are so beautiful. I want to lick you for the rest of the night, but as you know, we have to get ready for dinner."

"I know." She got off the bed. "Kiss me again and I'll see you downstairs."

Corrine gladly kissed her, softly and lovingly. Her head was spinning, and every nerve in her body was on alert when the kiss finally ended.

Katie left the room, and Corrine once again scrubbed her scent off. She put on black slacks, a purple vest, and gray coat and hurried downstairs.

"Oh, good. You're down before Katie. Not that that should surprise me. That child has no sense of time. I declare, I don't know what she does in that room that takes her so long."

"Did you need to talk to me?"

"I wanted to let you know that you and Katie will be home alone tomorrow, and I just wanted to be sure that would be acceptable to you."

Corrine's heart threatened to fly out of her chest. "Why would that be?"

"I received notice today. Theodore's brother is taking me to town to meet with the estate attorney."

"Is everything okay? Would you like me to accompany you?"

"Thank you, Cori, but no. Edward will take me and will represent me with the lawyer."

Before Corrine could say another word, Katie descended the stairs, looking like an angel in a yellow chiffon gown that brought out gold highlights in her hair and showed off her youthful glow.

"You look striking," Corrine said when Katie reached the bottom of the stairs.

"Thank you. You look very nice yourself."

They smiled at each other, then Corrine turned to Della. "Shall we see about dinner?"

When they were seated and dinner was served, Corrine asked, "What time will you be leaving tomorrow, Della?"

Katie's head snapped up. "You're going somewhere?"

"I was telling Cori that I need to go to town tomorrow. Your Uncle Edward will pick me up at ten o'clock. I'll be gone most of the day. I'm glad you have work to do so you won't be bored."

"We'll be fine." Corrine tried to sound calm while her pulse raced at the idea of several hours alone with Katie.

"And don't worry," Katie said. "I promise not to torment Miss Corrine too much."

"Miss Corrine?" Della arched an eyebrow.

"I meant to speak with you," Corrine said. "Miss Staples just seems so formal with us working together and spending so much time in each other's company. I suggested she call me that. I hope that's not a problem."

"I have no qualms with it. I think it makes good sense. I'm happy you two are getting along."

"We really are," Corrine said. "Now, if you'll excuse me, I need to tend to some of my business, so I'll retire to my room. I'll see you both in the morning."

Corrine was looking over some paperwork she'd brought with her, but she couldn't focus. Her ears perked at every sound, wondering if it was Katie on her way to bed. She hoped Katie would stop by her room and was disappointed when she didn't.

Midnight arrived and Corrine finally turned off the lamp and got ready for bed. Sleep escaped her for several hours as she lay there thinking about the morrow.

She awoke groggy at just past eight. She quickly donned her dressing gown and went downstairs in search of coffee. She carried the steaming mug to the breakfast nook where Della was relaxing.

"You look horrible this morning," Della said.

"Why, thank you."

"How late were you working last night?"

"I went to bed at midnight but had a hard time falling asleep."

"You should have slept later this morning. I appreciate your dedication, but you need to take care of yourself."

"I may go back to bed later," Corrine said, having every intention of taking Katie with her when she did.

Della and Corrine talked while they ate, and Corrine continued drinking coffee. The time passed quickly, and soon Della had to excuse herself to get ready for her trip to town.

Corrine took her coffee to the office where she found Katie concentrating on a ledger.

"I think I found something," she said when Corrine walked in. She looked up. "You're still in your dressing gown?"

"I didn't sleep well last night."

"Why not?"

"I was too excited about spending another day alone with you."

"It will be fun, won't it?"

"What did you say before? You think you found something?"

"Yes. Come look. This was from eight months ago. Incoming monies minus expenses equal an incorrect amount."

Corrine bent closer, aware of her body brushing against Katie's, but she remained determined to focus on the numbers. She saw that Katie's calculations indicated that the amount left over should have been eighteen hundred dollars, but the amount in the ledger was fifteen hundred.

"Three hundred dollars is a lot of money. Of course, that could have been an honest error. Let's make a note of that and check the next month."

"Should we tell my mother?"

"Not yet. Let's wait until we see a pattern."

She stood upright and looked down at Katie, whose gaze was roaming all over her body.

"Thoughts?" Corrine asked.

"I want to feel your body on me."

"I just want to feel your body."

"My body wants you to feel it."

Corrine fought with every muscle not to bend over and kiss Katie's perfect mouth. She was glad she didn't when Della walked in.

"Edward's coach is here, so I'll be taking my leave. Do either of you need anything from town?"

They shook their heads.

"Very well. Don't work too hard and I'll see you this evening."

CHAPTER TWELVE

Corrine stood over Katie, staring toward the front of the house. She heard the front door close, and she cut through the front room to watch the carriage pull away. She walked back to the office and found Katie standing, waiting for her.

"She's gone," Corrine said.

Katie smiled and stepped into Corrine's arms. Corrine closed the door to the office and kissed Katie. Their kiss grew more frantic as their hunger increased. Katie moved her hands under Corrine's dressing gown and ran them over her undershirt.

Corrine felt her body respond to Katie's touch. She kissed her harder and hiked up Katie's skirts to feel her nakedness underneath.

"You're so inviting," she said.

"I want you in me."

"I have to be in you." She pulled away and lowered Katie's dress. "Let's go upstairs."

They opened the door and, certain they were unobserved, they sneaked out of the office and up to Katie's room. Once safely behind closed doors, they had their arms around each other again, tongues dancing to the rhythm of their passion.

Corrine unbuttoned Katie's dress, then broke the kiss to peel the dress off and leave Katie standing in her corset. She roughly grabbed her breasts and sucked one nipple then the other. She licked the hardened nubs and rubbed her cheeks against the soft, smooth skin.

"Damn, Katie, I swear I can't get enough of you. I wish you could be naked around me every moment of the day so I could ravish your body whenever the notion hits. Your body is amazing."

She spun Katie around and untied her corset, then pulled it over Katie's head and tossed it on the floor. She pulled Katie to her and kissed her again, running her hands over her bare flesh.

Katie took Corrine's dressing gown off and lifted her nightshirt over her head. They kissed, their naked bodies pressed into each other.

Katie broke the kiss and walked over to the bed, swaying her hips as she walked.

"You know how I love that ass," Corrine said. "And it drives me mad to see it move like that."

Katie bent over and rested her head on the bed, leaving her ass on display for Corrine.

Corrine's cunt throbbed so hard it ached. She crossed the room and dropped to her knees. She pried Katie's legs apart and buried her tongue inside her while she squeezed and massaged her firm cheeks.

Katie bent her knees and lowered herself onto Corrine's tongue. She rubbed back and forth on her face, while Corrine's tongue moved on her and in her.

Corrine closed her mouth on Katie's clit and sucked the tiny morsel briefly before she stood and turned Katie over, lying on her and kissing her, sharing her juices with her.

She sat on the bed and helped Katie climb up on it. Katie lay on her back and bent her knees, letting her legs fall open.

Knowing how she liked to be looked upon, Corrine held Katie's legs wide by running her hands over her inner thighs. She pressed them out and gazed at the wet cunt exposed to her.

"I swear I can watch you swell simply by looking at you."

"I'm not surprised. If I had my way, I'd have you always staring at me."

Keeping her focus on Katie, Corrine placed three fingers against her opening. She slowly slid them inside, watching as Katie's twat swallowed them. She watched them reappear as she pulled them out, then disappear again as she pushed them back in.

Katie reached down and spread her lips so Corrine could see every inch of her. Corrine rubbed Katie's clit with her free hand, dragging her thumb over it and pressing it into her. She never wanted to stop playing in Katie's private playground. She was wet and hot and tight. Corrine pulled her hand away, then entered her with four fingers. She twisted her hand and pulled it back out. She buried her hand inside again and moved it in and out, going deeper with each thrust. She finally put her whole hand inside Katie's dripping cunt and made a fist, pummeling Katie's tender insides.

She moved her fist one way then the other as much as she could inside the tight confines of Katie. She continued rubbing her clit and fucking Katie until Katie's eyes closed, and she relaxed, giving herself completely to Corrine.

Corrine could barely keep her thumb on Katie's clit it was so slick, but she continued to rub her, first along her hard underside and then over her tip. Katie arched her hips and rotated them, pressing her clit into Corrine. Corrine watched as Katie absently played with her nipples while she fucked her.

Katie moved her hands off her tits and grabbed the bedspread as her bucking stopped and she cried out as the orgasms washed over her. Her cunt closed over and over on Corrine's hand, shooting her come down her arm.

"Oh, my," Katie said when she could find her voice. "That was amazing."

She licked her dry lips while Corrine licked her wet ones.

Katie placed her hand on the back of Corrine's head and forced her closer as she rotated her hips against her. It took no time at all for her to climax again, shuddering against Corrine's face.

Corrine kissed up Katie's body, pausing to suck on her nipples, then nibbled her neck, and finally claimed her mouth with her own. She pressed her knee into Katie, who groaned at the contact.

Katie moved her hand to between Corrine's legs and slipped her fingers inside. Corrine rode her hand while they kissed until she could no longer focus on anything but the way Katie was filling her.

She rolled off Katie and spread wide while Katie continued to fill her. Katie moved between her legs and licked at her clit while she moved her hand in and out.

Corrine reached her hand down and closed it around Katie's wrist. She made Katie's hand pump harder. She drove it in far, then pulled it out fast and plunged it in deeper. She picked up her speed until Katie relaxed her arm and let Corrine use her to fuck herself.

Corrine lost the ability to think, she was only aware of the sensations between her legs. She kept hammering her cunt until she felt the explosion build at her very core just before the heat shot out over every inch of her, the orgasm racking her body over and over.

"I loved the feel of my cunt closing around your fingers."

"That was incredible. I want always to fuck you that hard."

"Please do, sweetheart." Corrine grabbed Katie and pulled her to her. "As long as you fuck me, I care about little else."

She rolled over onto Katie again, pressing herself against Katie. Her clit, still sensitive, rubbed against Katie's while they kissed slowly and softly.

The kiss was interrupted by a knock on the door.

"Shh," Corrine whispered. "Whoever it is will go away."

Much to their dismay, the door opened as Mollie said, "Katie, darlin—" She stopped and stared at them on the bed. Her face was crimson. "What the hell is going on here?"

Corrine looked from Mollie to Katie and back. Mollie wasn't embarrassed; she was furious. The fact wasn't lost on Corrine.

Mollie spun and left the room, slamming the door behind her. Corrine slid off Katie.

"What was that all about?"

"She had no right to come in here without my permission."

"It sure seemed like she was comfortable entering your bedroom when she wanted. What do you suppose she was after? She sounded like she was hoping for a romp."

Corrine was out of bed, hurriedly getting dressed.

"Cori, what are you so upset about?"

"Who else are you fucking around here? Just so I know."

"You're being unreasonable."

"Am I? So I really am just an experiment, aren't I? And to think I was hoping to give my heart to you. What a fool I am."

"I told you I'd been with two women. Mollie happened to be one of them."

"You say that in the past tense. It sure didn't seem like she knew it was in the past."

"She's no right reacting that way. There was never anything serious between us."

"What about me? Should I assume we're serious? Or am I to believe we're just having fun?"

"I'm very serious about you. You know that."

"I want to believe that."

Katie got dressed. "I'll go talk to her."

"Why do you need to go talk to her?"

"I want to make sure she knows not to tell a soul what she saw."

Corrine sank down on the bed. "Oh, for God's sake. I hadn't thought about that."

"I'll be back as soon as I can."

❖

Katie found Mollie crying in her quarters in a building behind the main house.

"I suppose you've come to apologize." Mollie sobbed.

"I am sorry you had to see us. I should have said something," Katie said.

"Is it that easy for you to turn off what we had?"

"What we had was fun, Mollie. But there was no future."

"Three years, Katie. We've been making love for three years now. Forgive me for thinking you cared about me."

"I'm sorry if I misled you and I apologize for hurting you."

"As if that's going to make it all better."

"There's another reason I came here," Katie said. "That's to make sure you know not to mention what you saw to anybody."

"Why? It wouldn't do for the mistress of the house to know her best friend's fucking her daughter?"

"No, it would not do. And I'd hate to see what happened to you and your family should this get out."

"Are you threatening me, Katie Prentiss?"

"Call it what you will. I'm dead serious though. I don't want you saying anything to anyone."

Katie left Mollie and hurried back to her room, which she found empty. She walked down the hall to Corrine's room, but that too was empty. The reality of what happened was starting to sink in. Damned Mollie might have ruined her relationship with Corrine. She had to find her. She rushed downstairs to the office, but Corrine wasn't there either.

In a panic, Katie ran out of the house and found Corrine sitting on the side porch. She said nothing when Katie sat next to her.

"Cori, please talk to me."

"I want to believe this hasn't been a game to you, but how can I be sure?"

"I'm not playing a game. I care deeply for you. You must believe me."

"Walk with me." She stood.

"What?"

"I said, come on. Get up and walk with me to the stables. We need to talk."

Katie hurried down the porch steps and caught up with Corrine already crossing the lawn.

"At least you're speaking to me."

"I'm speaking for now. I make no promises what more I'll do."

"Will you listen as well as speak?"

"I'll try. I'm still not happy with you."

They entered the stables and walked to a pile of hay in the corner. They sat on the soft pile, and Katie stared intently at Corrine, who stared at her feet.

"Please talk to me. I can't bear for you to be upset with me."

Corrine raised her gaze to meet Katie's. "If we're to pursue this, I'll need complete honesty from you. I need to know I can trust you, and frankly, that won't be easy."

"But I've done nothing for you not to trust. I understand that you see it differently, but please believe me. I had no intention of seeing Mollie again once I learned of your feelings for me."

"So you say. But what I know is that you did nothing to prove that. Had I not been in your room and she came calling, how am I to know you wouldn't have opened your legs for her?"

"I'm telling you that, and I've not lied to you."

"Why didn't you tell her you didn't want to see her anymore?"

"I didn't think about it. I didn't feel obligated to her. We had sex when we were bored or aroused. I never considered her my sweetheart and I knew it would end sometime. When you and I got together, I didn't even think that I needed to tell her."

"I hear what you're saying, but I can't say it makes me more comfortable. That girl obviously cared deeply for you. To you, she was nothing more than a plaything. How do I know I'm any different?"

"You are different! I never had feelings for her. And in my defense, she never told me she had feelings for me either."

"I suppose that does put you in a better light. What would you have done if she had declared her love for you?"

"I hadn't thought about it. I suppose I would have told her I didn't have those feelings for her. You've got to know me well enough to know I'm not a monster. I don't go around trying to hurt people."

"I would very much like to believe that."

"Cori…" Katie placed her hand on Corrine's arm. Corrine stiffened and pulled away.

"Please don't be that way," Katie said. "I can't bear the thought of my life without you. I declare, you're the only bright spot in my world."

"It's not easy for me to turn my feelings on and off."

"I'm sorry. I am truly sorry that I hurt you. I hope never to do that again. I just pray you'll give me another chance."

"Please understand my confusion. Even as I'm wary of being a victim of some game you are playing, your body this close to me ignites my senses. This isn't easy."

"Don't fight it." She leaned her body against Corrine's. "Please let yourself experience all your desires."

"Unfortunately, my heart is yet to be convinced."

Katie took Corrine's hand and placed it on her breast. "Feel this and tell me you don't want it. Tell your heart it's safe with me."

CHAPTER THIRTEEN

The feel of Katie's soft skin had Corrine light-headed. Desire warred with common sense. She wanted to take Katie again but knew she wouldn't be able to separate her heart from her lust. If she made love to Katie then, she'd be surrendering her soul to Katie to do with as she pleased.

She stared at Katie's tear-stained face, her swollen eyes pleading with Corrine for another chance. Corrine's resolve weakened. Every ounce of her wanted to trust Katie. She leaned forward and took Katie's soft lips between hers. The kiss was brief but monumental. It said more than any words could.

Katie smiled then pulled Corrine back to her. Their kissing escalated, and Corrine soon had Katie's skirt around her waist and her fingers inside her. She was on her back with Katie straddling her, riding her fingers. They kissed while Katie continued to move on her until her crotch closed tightly around Corrine's fingers.

They got Katie put back together and walked to the house. When they were in Corrine's room, she made a point of locking the door before crossing the room to take Katie in her arms.

"Look me in the eye. Promise me you feel this too."

"I do, Cori. I swear to you I do."

They stripped each other's clothes off and collapsed on the bed. Limbs tangled with limbs, tongues roamed over every exposed inch, fingers explored hidden depths.

Corrine couldn't get enough of Katie. She feasted on every inch of her and was rewarded as Katie came repeatedly for her. She gave her body and soul to Katie, and Katie claimed her with the confidence of one who knew her lover. She moved hard and fast against and inside Corrine, and Corrine responded to every touch.

They lay in each other's arms, satiated and serene, when they heard hooves clopping outside.

Corrine sat up. "Your mother's home. Hurry. Get dressed."

Katie slipped into her dress and scurried to her room. Corrine quickly washed up and dressed for dinner. She went downstairs to see Della looking tired and gaunt.

"Are you not feeling well, Della?"

"I fear I've got a bug. I'll be fine. I wonder if Katie is about ready for dinner."

Corrine was concerned. "You look exhausted. How did everything go?"

"It went well. Theodore had investments I wasn't aware of. Edward knew of these investments, so we met with the attorney to discuss them. It was fine."

"I'm glad Theodore left you in good shape."

"I would have expected nothing less." She looked to the top of the stairs. "Ah, there's Katie. Shall we eat?"

When they were seated, Della stared hard at Katie. "Katie, dear, are you feeling well?"

"I'm fine, Mama. Why do you ask?"

"You look a little flushed. And your eyes look bloodshot."

"It must be from looking at those ledgers all day."

"I told you not to work too hard."

"I promise I didn't."

Corrine couldn't suppress a smile. Truer words were never spoken.

❖

Wednesday morning, Katie sat next to Corrine in the office. "I'm so glad we worked things out yesterday," she said.

"Me too. I wasn't fond of the idea that we were over."

"You certainly scared me."

"Just promise you'll always be honest with me. That's all I ask."

"Have you been hurt before?"

"I've never let anyone close enough to hurt me."

"That's sad."

Corrine laughed. "It's suited me well."

"What about the woman you told me about that night in New Orleans?"

"That woman was you."

"You said you loved her."

"I do."

Katie's eyes shone with understanding. "You do? Oh, Cori. I love you, too. Thank you so much for letting me close."

"I'd like very much to have you close always."

"That can be arranged." Katie moved against Corrine and kissed her.

"Is it your hope to get us caught again?" Corrine smiled.

"I'm sorry. I just can't keep my hands and lips off you."

"I love having your hands and lips all over me."

"When do you think we'll get to make love again?"

"I think another fishing trip will be in order on Sunday."

"But that's such a long way off," Katie whined.

"Time will go faster if we keep busy. Now grab a ledger and let's look for more discrepancies."

They found several more mistakes in the ledgers, too many to be coincidental. By late afternoon, Corrine was certain Paddy Flanagan had been skimming money from Della. She and Katie were discussing telling her when Della came into the office.

"Cori, may I have a word with you, please?"

Corrine followed her into the day room. "What can I do for you?"

Della wrung her hands as she paced. "This isn't easy for me."

"What isn't?"

"You know how servants talk."

Corrine felt the cold fist of fear in the pit of her stomach. "Of course."

"I just overheard two of them talking. They were saying Mollie Flanagan caught you and Katie in bed together."

Corrine was nauseated. She had no response.

"I'm not saying I believe what they were saying, and I'm not asking you to confirm or deny it at this moment. I'm simply saying I've been a good friend and have tolerated your odd ways all these years. I've never understood them, but I've tolerated them. What I won't tolerate is you corrupting the only daughter I have."

"Della, I—"

"That's all. I've said my piece. I trust you to act based on my wishes. I'd hate to have to ask you to leave." She fell into a coughing fit, and Corrine left the room and went up to her bedroom.

An hour later, she was still lying on her bed replaying everything that had happened in the weeks she'd been visiting. A knock on her door interrupted her musing. Her body felt like lead as she hefted herself off the bed. She opened the door to find Katie standing there.

"Why didn't you come back to the office?"

Corrine turned away from her without answering.

"Cori? What is it? What's wrong?"

Corrine sat heavily on the bed and placed her hands on her knees. She forced herself to look Katie in the eye. "Your mother knows about us."

"She what? How?" She broke into a bright smile. "Wait, who cares how? Don't you see? This is a good thing."

"I fail to see any good in it."

"No more sneaking around. We can be open. This is wonderful news."

"I'm afraid it won't work that way."

"Why not? I feel so relieved! Why aren't you happy?"

"She overheard some servants talking. She told me she'll not have me corrupting her daughter."

"What? Corrupting? Did you tell her I'm an adult and am participating of my own accord?"

"I did not."

"You didn't deny it, did you? You didn't opt to hide what we have, did you?"

"I tried to talk to her, but she didn't want to hear it. She simply said not to corrupt you."

"So what does this mean? Don't tell me you're going to honor her wishes."

"It seems like the right thing to do."

"The right thing? How can you say such nonsense? There's nothing right about that. I'm going to tell her the truth and tell her that she has no say in whether we continue to see each other."

Corrine grabbed her arm. "Don't."

"Why not? You're choosing her over me, aren't you? I thought you said you wouldn't do that."

"Katie, she's threatening to send me away."

"What? No! Oh, Lord, Cori, I wouldn't know what to do if you weren't here with me."

"I've yet to make up my mind what I shall do."

"You're not going anywhere! I'm going to go speak with her now. She needs to understand that this is serious. It's not some dalliance. She'll see then that she can't send you away."

"Please don't do that. You didn't see her. She was not playing at telling me to leave. She will do so if she discovers we truly are carrying on."

Katie seethed inside. Her mother and Corrine were being unreasonable, but she sensed there was no point arguing with them. She needed to do something, though. She felt helpless and didn't like that feeling.

She stormed out of the room and came face to face with Mollie.

"You bitch!" she screamed as she slapped Mollie across the face with all her might.

The force of the blow sent Mollie sprawling backward across a table, knocking a vase to the floor. The priceless vase shattered, but Katie paid it no mind. She stood over Mollie and yelled at her.

"I warned you not to open your big mouth. But you just had to, didn't you? Couldn't keep it shut, could you?"

The commotion brought several people running. Servants huddled at the end of the hallway. Corrine came rushing out of her room, and Katie's mother was up the stairs in a heartbeat and grabbed the rail as she gasped for breath.

Corrine was the first to reach Katie and wrapped her arms around her from behind, pulling her away from the bruised and bawling Mollie, collapsed to the floor.

"Katie, that won't do!" Corrine said. "What are you thinking?"

Katie spun out of Corrine's grip and right into her mother, who was staring at her in disbelief.

"What's gotten into you, child?"

Katie was still livid and did not bother to think before she spoke. "Cori's not corrupting me! I'll have you know I was fucking this slut"—she pointed at Mollie—"for years before Cori came to visit."

Katie realized what she said and knew she'd never be able to take the words back. She tried to gloss over it. "And her father's stealing from you."

She stormed down the hall and slammed her bedroom door. Corrine stood staring at Della, at a loss for what to say.

"Get this mess cleaned up," Della said to Mollie before going back downstairs.

Corrine remained in the hallway, torn about what to do. She wanted to go after Katie but was too angry to deal with her right then. She knew she needed to talk to Della but dreaded that like the plague. She moved to help Mollie to her feet, but she shied away and shook her head.

"I'll thank you not to touch me."

"I was just going to help you."

"You've done more than enough for me, ma'am."

Corrine knew there was no more putting off the confrontation with Della. She found her in the office staring at the ledgers.

"Does any of that make sense to you?" Corrine asked.

"Nothing is making sense to me these days." Della's body was racked with a coughing fit.

Corrine waited until the coughing subsided. "Della, I'm sorry."

Della put her hand up to silence her. "Is it true Paddy was stealing from me?"

"Yes."

"How much?"

"I don't have the exact number. Several thousand dollars anyway. Are you sure you're okay? Health wise, I mean."

"I'm fine. And it's no concern to you, at any rate. About Paddy, I suppose I should have him arrested."

"And what of his family?"

"These are decisions I must make. Now is when I need a best friend to talk to. Preferably one not having an affair with my daughter."

"I understand that you're upset."

"You understand nothing." She turned in her chair to face Corrine. "You came into my house bringing all your deviant desires and set your sights on my daughter. This is Katie we're talking about. The little girl you used to carry on your shoulders. How long have you been planning this? Does your type like little girls too? Has bedding her always been a goal of yours?"

"It's never been a goal of mine. It just happened. I never dreamed I'd fall in love with her."

"In love? You're telling me you love my Katie?"

"I do. And she feels the same."

"Is this supposed to make me feel better? Because I feel more nauseous every moment."

"I just want you to be aware this wasn't some casual affair."

"Katie's young. She has a future ahead of her. She'll find a nice young man and settle down. She'll give me grandchildren to play with in my old age."

"Even if I wasn't in her life, it doesn't mean she'll suddenly prefer men."

"Believe what you will. I want you out of our lives immediately."

"Have you stopped to think how happy Katie's been lately?"

"Of course she's happy. She's having her fancy tickled by my former best friend. It's no wonder you've been telling me you enjoy her company. What a fool I was not to know you meant her company in your bed."

"Damn it, Della! I'm trying to tell you, there's more to it than that. Katie will be as bereft as I if I leave."

"Pardon me for not feeling any sympathy. She'll get over you. She'll soon realize you were but a passing fancy for her."

"But I'm not."

"I believe you are. Now pack your things. I want you out of my house by sundown."

With heavy heart, Corrine climbed the stairs and walked down the hall to Katie's room. She knocked on the door, but there was no answer. She tried the knob, but it was locked.

"Katie? It's me. May I come in?"

"I want to be alone," came the muffled answer.

Determined to talk to her later, Corrine went to her room and pulled her trunk from under the bed. She stood in front of her wardrobe and stared blankly at the clothes hanging there. She was numb when she finally started taking clothes down and folding them into her trunk. The wardrobe was half-empty when she heard her door open.

She turned to see Katie standing there, tears pouring down her cheeks. "What's going on? What are you doing?"

"Your mother has told me to leave. I can't say I'm surprised. I warned you this would happen if she found out about us. I'm still quite shocked you felt the need to confirm her suspicions."

"I wasn't thinking. I was so upset. I'm sorry I said anything."

"I'm sorry too. And now I must take my leave."

"I don't want you to." She threw herself in Corrine's arms.

"Oh, sweetheart, I don't want to leave, either. But I can't stay." She kissed Katie's head.

"Can you stay in New Orleans?"

"If I'm not here with you, New Orleans would be far too lonely."

"But Baton Rouge is so far away."

"It might do well for me to leave so you can move on with your life."

"I don't want to move on. I want you, Cori. She can't do this to us!"

"I'm afraid she can and she has." She pulled away. "Have a seat while I continue packing."

Katie sat on the bed and watched as Corrine put clothes in the trunk.

"When will I see you again?" Katie asked.

"I don't know."

"But I will see you again, right?"

"Let me take some time to think things out. Perhaps I'll formulate a plan. Right now, I'm not thinking clearly."

"I hate my mother."

"No, you don't. She's trying to do what she thinks is best."

"But it's not."

"We'll get through this. For now, I need you to take care of her. She's not well."

"I know. I think it's all this mourning."

"I think it's more than that. Her cough is getting worse."

"Why should I take care of her after what she's doing to us?"

"Because she's your mother. And she loves you."

"She has a strange way of showing it."

Corrine turned to look at Katie. She tilted her head up and lightly brushed her lips. "I'll miss you, darling."

Katie pulled at Corrine. "Lay with me."

"I can't."

Katie untucked Corrine's shirt and unbuttoned her trousers.

"Katie, please…"

"I need you one more time before you leave."

"Certainly, you can't feel aroused at a time like this."

"Nothing stops me from wanting you, Cori. Nothing ever will."

Corrine kissed her hard, her own need rising at Katie's words.

Katie peeled Corrine's pants off and moved her hand between her legs. She stroked her clit, coaxing it to grow. She played with her lips and finally slid her fingers inside.

"Easy there, love." Corrine took her shirt off and kissed Katie again while she unbuttoned her dress. Together, they took it off and Corrine sucked greedily on her breasts while she untied her corset.

When they were both free from clothing, Corrine lay on top of Katie and moaned at the feel of Katie's flesh under her.

"Your skin is so soft. I want to memorize every inch of you."

She nibbled on Katie's neck, pausing briefly to suck her earlobe.

Katie squirmed against Corrine, fueling her desire. Corrine kissed down Katie, stopping briefly to lick and tug each nipple before she continued her path to the heaven where Katie's legs met.

She spread Katie's legs and placed soft kisses on her swollen clit. She dragged her tongue over every bit of her pleasure zone.

"I'll never forget the taste of you. You are delicious," she said before burying her tongue deep to lick the special spot that made Katie quiver. She moved her mouth back to Katie's clit and put her fingers inside to stroke her.

She looked up and saw Katie playing with her nipples, and she sucked harder and pumped faster until she felt Katie's body tremble under her. When her breathing was close to normal, she took her in her arms and held her tight.

Katie pulled free and bit one of Corrine's nipples while she put her hand between her legs. She drove three fingers inside Corrine and spread them apart as she pulled them out. She slipped four fingers back in and moved them in and out as fast and hard as she could.

"Damn, girl, you feel good." Corrine groaned, arching her hips to take each thrust as deeply as she could. She couldn't think, only feel as the lights started going off behind her eyelids and the explosions rocked her body.

Katie climbed back into Corrine's arms and snuggled against her. She couldn't stop the tears that rolled out of her eyes.

"Oh, sweetheart, please don't cry."

"What if you meet someone else when you leave here?"

"I'd gone thirty-seven years without meeting someone before I fell for you. Chances are pretty good I won't meet anybody else."

"I can't bear not seeing you every day."

"Katie, please. Let's not do this. Let's let our last moments be happy, basking in the warmth of our lovemaking."

Katie rolled over and buried her face in Corrine's shoulder. "I can't help it." She sobbed.

Corrine held her while she cried, fighting tears herself.

CHAPTER FOURTEEN

The sound of Della's cough in the hall roused them. "She's no doubt looking for you," Corrine said.

"It would serve her right to walk in here and see us."

"I don't think so, sweetheart. Come on. We have to get up."

They were dressed with Katie on the bed and Corrine finishing her packing when they heard a knock on the door.

"Come in," Corrine called.

Della entered the room and did not acknowledge Corrine. To Katie, she said, "I feared I'd find you here. Dinner's ready."

"I'm not hungry."

"That matters not. You'll go change for dinner."

"I won't."

"Young lady, I'm your mother and you will listen to me. Leave this room immediately."

"No."

Della looked at Corrine. "Thank you so much for all you've done for us."

Katie stood and looked at her mother. "What's that supposed to mean? She's done wonderful things for us. And she was your best friend until she dared care for me."

Della doubled over as a coughing spasm tore through her.

"Della, perhaps you should see a doctor."

"Perhaps you should mind your own business. For a change." Della stood upright and looked at Katie. "I'll see you downstairs in ten minutes."

"No, you won't." Katie sat back on the bed as her mother slammed the door on her way out.

"I worry about her health."

"She gets what she deserves."

"Katie, that's not nice. I'm serious."

"She does look horrible, doesn't she?"

"Promise me you'll call for the doctor."

"Part of me knows I should, but part of me doesn't want to do anything for her."

"She's your mother. And it would be a favor to me if you did."

"Why don't you stay and call for her?"

"Nice try, sweetheart." She closed the lid of her trunk. "That's it. I suppose we should say good-bye here."

"Nonsense. I'll see you out. I'll watch until I can no longer see the coach."

Corrine wiped a tear from Katie's cheek. "I'll never stop loving you, Katie Prentiss."

"Nor I you. Please come up with a plan for us soon."

"I shall do my best, my love. You have my word." She kissed Katie softly and deeply, wanting to leave her impression on her lips forever.

Hand in hand, they left the room and walked down the stairs. The coach was waiting, and Corrine sent the driver in to retrieve her trunk. She looked up at the house and checked each window. There was no sign of Della. Her heart ached for hurting her. It ached for having to leave Katie. She was surprised it hadn't broken in half.

Movement in one window caught her attention, but she was crushed to see Mollie's face.

"It looks as though someone is happy to see me leaving," she told Katie, who looked up and extended her middle finger to Mollie.

Corrine laughed but tried to sound serious. "That wasn't very ladylike."

"I hate her."

"I hope you'll remember that once I'm gone."

"Oh, you have my word. I'll never be with anyone but you ever again. And I'll especially not be with her."

"I do hope your mother sends that whole family away. I'll be more comfortable then."

The coachman was back with the trunk. He stood waiting for Corrine.

"This is it then."

Katie threw her arms around Corrine's neck. "Please don't go."

Corrine wrapped her arms around Katie and held her close. "I wish I didn't have to. Promise me again you'll never forget me."

"Never," Katie said before kissing Corrine passionately in front of anyone who happened to see.

"I love you, Katie. I always will."

"Please come back soon. I feel I'm losing a part of me."

"I know I am. I'm leaving my heart here."

Corrine kissed her once more, then climbed in the coach. She faced the mansion and waved to Katie even as she receded out of sight.

Katie walked into the house to find her mother in the living room. "I do hope this nonsense is over now," her mother said.

Katie looked at her. She was obviously sick. Katie noted her pallor and weight loss. "It's not nonsense. By the way, she made me promise to call for the doctor."

"I don't take instructions from her."

"She loves you. You should know that."

"I'm not her type."

"That wasn't fair."

"It's true."

"So is this how it will be? You'll torment me until what? I apologize for loving her? I'm sorry you lost your best friend, but it was your own doing, and you'd better not try to blame it on me."

"I don't blame you for anything, Katie. You're a child."

"I'm not a child. It's high time you realize that."

"You are a child, and she took advantage of you. If a lady can't trust her child with her best friend, something's very wrong."

"How can you sit there so calmly and spew such balderdash?"

"I'll thank you to watch your language. I fear I have quite a journey ahead of me to get you back to acting like a lady."

"I'll start acting like a lady when you stop treating me like a child." She went upstairs to her room, threw herself on the bed, and cried herself to sleep.

❖

Corrine spent the night in New Orleans, as there was no steamship leaving until the morning. She passed the night in a pub until she stumbled to her rented room in the early morning hours. Later that morning, head heavy from too much whiskey, she lay in her bed staring at the ceiling. If only the pounding in her head would outweigh the pain in her heart.

The boat ride was long but uneventful. She sat quietly, ignoring everything around her, lost in her thoughts and her longing for Katie. When the twelve-hour ride was over, she hired a coach at the pier to take her the short distance to her house where she also kept her office. Her home felt small and cramped compared to the vastness of the plantation house. And it felt unbearably empty without Katie.

She spent the next two days in bed, too heartsick to do anything but sleep. When Sunday arrived, she made herself presentable and walked into town to get some food. She crossed into the restaurant area and was greeted by a newsboy hawking his papers.

"Read all about it. Lincoln wins the election!"

"What's that?" She crossed the street and bought a paper.

"There's already talk of secession," the boy said as he handed over the newspaper.

"Thank you," Corrine said absently as she looked over the story. She tucked the paper under her arm and entered a restaurant where she read the front-page article and waited for her biscuits and gravy.

It was over. The unthinkable had happened and Lincoln had won the election. She knew several states were thinking of seceding from the Union. She wondered what Louisiana would do. And how all this would affect Katie and the plantation. She knew Katie had dreaded this result. She desperately wanted to be with her, to console her and assure her all would be well, even as she feared the end of the country as they knew it.

Her breakfast arrived and she felt nauseated. She fought the urge to push the plate away. She needed nourishment, regardless of how unappealing food sounded. It was time to let the idyllic days of the plantation go and get back to business on the docks. She would need her strength to keep up.

Monday morning, Katie walked into the office to find Paddy Flanagan seated at her father's desk. Her blood boiled at the sight of him.

"What do you think you're doing?"

Paddy stood. "I heard Mrs. Prentiss's friend left. Since she was seeing to the books, I thought I'd better have a look at them with her gone."

"I'll be seeing to the books now. You and your family have already done enough damage."

"What's that supposed to mean?" he asked.

"You know exactly what it means. Your daughter's been running around causing trouble. And we know what you've been doing with the books. Now get out of this office immediately."

His normal ruddy complexion paled as he hastened past her and out the door. She watched him leave, then went in search of her mother. She wasn't in the day room or the breakfast nook. She poked her head in the kitchen and saw Paddy talking quietly to Abigail in the corner. It was Maddy she was looking for, and she saw her washing dishes.

"Maddy, have you seen my mother this morning?"

"No, ma'am, Miss Katie. She hasn't been down yet."

Thinking that odd, Katie climbed the stairs and went to her mother's room. There was no answer to her knock, so she opened the door. She found her mother lying there, covered in sweat.

"Mama, you look horrible. You're so pale. You're not well. I'm sending for a doctor."

Her mother didn't argue but lay quietly, her glassy eyes barely focused. Katie hurried down the stairs and into the kitchen. "Maddy. Go have your brother ride to town to fetch Dr. Logan. My mother is quite ill and needs to be seen immediately. Now go!"

She went back upstairs and filled a basin of water and grabbed a washrag. She sat on the bed and placed the cool towel on her mother's forehead. She took the towel off, dipped it in the cool water, and repeated.

"Mama, how did you let yourself get this bad?"

"If you're trying to cheer me up, you're failing miserably." She coughed for a few minutes and tried to say something else but fell back onto her pillow, exhausted.

"Look at you. You're weak and feverish, and that cough certainly isn't improving. Dr. Logan should be here soon."

"I wish you hadn't sent for him. I'm sure this will pass."

"At the very least, he may give you some quinine to help quiet that cough."

Katie continued tending to her mother until Maddy's brother knocked on the door and had Dr. Logan in tow.

"Thank you, Jacques," Katie said. "Dr. Logan, thank you so much for coming to see my mother."

"I'm happy to have a look at her. Now if you'll excuse me, I'll need to speak with her alone."

Katie went to her room and sat on the cushions by the window, staring down at where the coach had taken Corrine away four days earlier. It seemed like forever, and now with her mother sick, Katie felt more alone than ever. She wanted Corrine here to tell her how to care for her mother. She would know these things. Corrine was smart like that.

Katie wiped away a tear as she hugged her knees to her chest and rocked. She wondered if Corrine still thought of her. And if she missed Katie nearly as much as Katie missed her.

She sat there for quite a while and began to wonder what Dr. Logan had discovered about her mother. She stepped into the hallway as Dr. Logan exited her mother's room. He looked somber, and her heart skipped a beat.

"What is it, Doctor? How is Mama?"

"It's not good, Katie. I'm afraid your mother has consumption."

'That's not good. I've heard of that. What can you do for her?"

"I'm sorry, but there's nothing I can do."

"But that sounds like she's going to die. She can't die. You can't let her die!" She fell into his arms, sobbing. Regardless of the fact that she had sent Corrine away, she was still Katie's mother, and Katie couldn't bear losing her, not this soon after losing her daddy to the Fever.

"I really am sorry, lass. It's only a matter of time now. Just keep her comfortable and see to it she has plenty of liquids. I've left some quinine to help with her cough, but outside of that, there's nothing I can do. I'll caution you to be careful around her, as consumption is highly contagious."

"So you're saying I could die too? I may as well. I have nothing to live for."

"Katie, I'll not stand idly by and listen to such ranting. You are young and have your whole life ahead of you. Please be careful around your mother. Don't spend any more time in there than necessary."

She saw him to the door, then walked back up to her mother's room. She needed Corrine so desperately. She didn't feel strong enough to watch her mother die alone. She let herself into her mother's room but saw she was sleeping, so she started to leave.

"Did you talk to Dr. Logan?" her mother asked weakly.

Katie fought back tears. "I did."

"Did he tell you I'm dying?"

"Oh, Mama, don't say such a thing."

"It's true, sweetheart. We need to accept it. And you can't get close to me."

"But I can't stay away from you." Fresh tears spilled from her eyes.

"You must. I'll not have you suffering with this. Dr. Logan is sending a nurse to care for me. You're not to do anything to put yourself in danger."

"No one else can care for you the way I can."

"I'd rather someone else be in danger. That's how it's going to be. Now, if you'll excuse me, I must sleep."

Katie watched her mother's eyes close and went back to her room where she lay down and cried.

CHAPTER FIFTEEN

Wednesday morning, Katie went into her mother's room to see how she was feeling. She was still sound asleep and drenched in perspiration. Katie decided not to wake her and went downstairs to have breakfast and work for a while instead.

As soon as she sat down in the breakfast nook, Maddy came bursting out of the kitchen. "They've gone, Miss Katie. When Abigail wasn't here by six o'clock, I went to fetch her, and their quarters were empty. There isn't anything left. They must have left in the middle of the night, because Abigail was here helping me with today's menu until ten o'clock or so."

Katie tried to absorb the information. Conflicting emotions washed over her. She was quite happy the troublesome family was gone, but she was mad as hell that Paddy wouldn't be facing charges. She was also livid that the family ran off without paying her family back for their fare from Ireland.

"Nobody saw them leave? Are you quite certain?"

"Yes, ma'am. No one saw them."

"Have Jacques check the stables to make sure no horses are missing. Tell him to report back to me. I'll be in the office."

She poured a cup of coffee and carried it into her favorite room. She could still feel Corrine's presence there and longed to have her sitting at the desk next to her, sneaking kisses and forbidden touches. She put her head in her hands and fought back new tears. It seemed all she did was cry of late.

"Miss Katie?" Jacques said from the door.

"Yes? What did you find?"

"They took your horse, ma'am. They took your horse and the roan and two saddlebags."

"You go directly to town, Jacques. Get the constable and have him come out here. We need to report this. I want the Flanagans arrested."

Jacques disappeared and Katie sat, exhausted from life. She wanted to crawl into bed, curl into a ball, and let the world move past her. If Corrine were there, she'd let her do that. She'd take care of everything. But she wasn't there, and Katie was in charge. She had never felt more alone.

Wanting to have things ready when the police arrived, she grabbed the ledgers that had the discrepancies she and Corrine had found. She stacked them neatly on the coffee table in the living room, then walked to the stables to verify Jacques's assessment.

Sure enough, Spirit was gone. His stall looked as empty as her heart felt. She went to investigate the saddlebags and found the one that held her father's fishing equipment missing. The one she and Corrine had used the week before when they had gone fishing. Had it only been a week? It seemed like forever since she and Corrine had lain naked together under the oaks and made love all day.

The thoughts weren't helping her mood, and she walked back to the house with a list of what was missing. She heard Maddy in the kitchen and stopped to have her make a tray for her to take to her mother.

Katie went upstairs carrying a tray of eggs, toast, and milk. She found her mother awake and sitting up.

"Are you feeling better, Mama?"

"I feel stronger this morning."

"Maybe you're getting better after all. Perhaps Dr. Logan was wrong."

She moved to set the tray on her mother's lap but stopped at the sight of blood on the front of her nightgown.

"Mother, you're bleeding."

"I must have coughed it up as I slept. After breakfast, I'll change out of this gown."

There was a knock on the door, and Katie opened it to find Pierre standing with a robust blond woman who looked to be a few years older than Katie.

"May I help you?" Katie asked, annoyed at the interruption.

"My name is Sarah Livingston. Dr. Logan sent me to care for your mother."

Relief washed over Katie. "Please come in." To Pierre, she said, "Please take Sarah's things to the spare room across the hall. She'll be staying there while she's taking care of my mother."

She walked Sarah to the bed. "This is my mother, Mrs. Della Prentiss. Mama, this is Sarah."

"I'm feeling much better today," her mother said. "I fear Dr. Logan might have been a bit hasty in his prognosis."

"I'm glad you're feeling well," Sarah said. "And I hope Dr. Logan was mistaken, but until we know for sure, I'll be tending to you."

There was another knock on the door, and this time it was Jacques and the constable. "Will you excuse me?" Katie said to her mother and Sarah.

"Not so fast," her mother said. "Why is the constable here?"

"Mama, I don't want to worry you. I have everything well in hand."

"Be that as it may, I'd like to know why the constable was brought to my home."

"The Flanagans have run off."

"The nerve!"

"And they took Spirit and the roan and some saddlebags. I'm going to file charges against them."

"Good girl. I want them brought to justice."

"You rest, Mama. I'll take care of this." Katie joined the men in the hall and closed the door behind her.

"Thank you, Jacques. That will be all." She led the constable down to the living room. "It all started a few months ago when my mother noticed the amount of money she was receiving from the plantation was less than normal. So she called on a friend of hers who is a bookkeeper by trade, and she and I went over the ledgers. We found that Paddy Flanagan was stealing money from us."

"How do you reckon it was him?"

"He took over the books when my father passed."

"I see. Did he know you suspected him?"

"I'm afraid I said something to that effect to him the other day."

"And now he's gone?"

"He and his family. And two of our horses and some saddlebags and my father's fishing equipment."

The officer jotted notes as Katie spoke. "And these ledgers are the ones that have proof he was stealing?" He pointed to the pile on the table.

"They do," Katie said.

"I'll need to take these with me."

"Please do."

"And why was this family here to begin with?"

"They were indentured servants. My father paid their passage from Ireland."

"How much longer did they have?"

"I can't be sure."

"I'll need you to find the records so we'll know how much they were in debt to you."

"Yes, sir. I'll be happy to."

"Can you describe them to me? What did they look like?"

"I fear it will be hard for me to be objective, but I shall try. Paddy was a short, round man with a bald head. Abigail, his wife, was a tall woman. Attractive, with shocking red hair. And their daughter Mollie was gorgeous. She was black Irish like her father. Her hair was long and dark and her eyes a deep brown."

The constable arched an eyebrow at the description but continued making notes.

"That's a pretty vague description, but we'll be on the lookout for any party of three that might match them."

"Thank you, sir. I do hope you'll find them."

"Me too. Now the boy you sent to find me described the horses to me as a fine black gelding and an older roan. Is that correct?"

"Yes, sir."

"That should do it for me. I'll be in touch if we find them."

"Thank you so much."

"I'm sorry you've had to go through this."

She walked him to the door and bid him good day, then went back up to her mother's room. She found Sarah sitting by the window, staring out over the plantation while her mother slept.

"I thought she was feeling better this morning," Katie said.

"She's still weak. She'll have days where she feels stronger, but I'm afraid that doesn't mean she's getting better."

Katie didn't appreciate her negativity. "So you'll just be here if she needs you?"

"That's correct. I'll track her fever and see to it she gets nourishment and liquids. It won't do for you to be in here where you can catch this."

"But you can catch it. Why do you do this?"

"It's what I love. I love caring for people."

"Surely you must have a family who worries about you spending all your time with the ill."

"I'm a spinster, Katie. I've no one waiting for me at home. This is what I do."

Katie's opinion softened. "Thank you for taking care of Mama. Did y'all get acquainted while I was downstairs?"

"We had a nice visit. She didn't know we'll have a new president, so we talked a little about that and about goings-on in the city."

"Who's president?"

"Abraham Lincoln. I declare, I don't know how you hadn't heard."

"We don't get away from here much."

"Bless your heart. You certainly have a lot on your young shoulders, Katie. I'm quite happy to be able to share the burden of your mother's care. At least with me here, you won't have to wait on her hand and foot. She knows you can't be in here, so you mustn't feel guilty. You tend to your business and I'll tend to her. Sound fair?"

"I don't know that I can stay away from her."

"I don't expect you never to see her. Just not often. Trust me, it's for the best. For now, why don't you go take some time for yourself? You've earned it."

Katie left the room feeling like she was abandoning her mother. She went to her room and lay down, the events of the past week running through her mind.

She rolled over and clutched her pillow to her chest, missing Corrine so much it hurt. She needed her strength to lean on and her body to enjoy. She wondered if Corrine was any closer to a plan for getting them back together. She didn't think she could bear another minute away from her.

It felt like the world was crumbling around her, and all she wanted was to lie in Corrine's arms and have her tell her that everything would be fine. She didn't want to be responsible for running the house and finding the Flanagans and caring for her mother all by herself. Sarah had instructed her to do something for herself. She could think of only one thing that was truly for her.

She sneaked into her father's room and helped herself to some shirts. She pulled a suitcase from under her bed and placed two pairs of riding breeches and the shirts in it. She opened her dressing table and removed the false bottom from a drawer. She found the money she'd been saving and put it in a handbag. She went downstairs and found Jacques in the kitchen talking to Maddy.

"Jacques, go hitch the carriage. I need you to drive me into town."

Jacques did as he was instructed, and soon Katie was on her way to New Orleans, the first step of her journey.

She arrived just in time and had Jacques stop the carriage on the landing by the large steamboat. She had him wait until she had her ticket purchased and had boarded the boat, then she sent him off with a wave.

She sat quietly, suitcase on her lap, avoiding the curious stares of fellow travelers. She hadn't considered how it would look to be traveling alone. More than once, she was approached by unsavory characters leering at her and hinting at services they hoped she provided.

The trip seemed to last forever, and she was relieved when she finally disembarked in Baton Rouge. It was early morning, but the dock was already alive. Men were loading ships and smoking tobacco and watching her. She held her head high and marched to the closest coach for hire.

"Do you know of the office of a Miss Corrine Staples?" she asked the driver.

"I do. Climb in."

He dropped her off in front of a small house with a shingle in front announcing Staples Bookkeeping. She stood on the darkened front step and pounded on the door as hard as she could.

❖

Corrine was tossing and turning, as was her norm of late. She'd had erotic dreams of Katie again and woke aroused and lonely. She heard the horse outside and was perplexed at the pounding on her door.

She peered out the window and couldn't believe her eyes. She threw the door open and grabbed Katie in a tight hug.

"What are you doing here?" She finally moved Katie back so she could look at her.

Katie burst into tears. "I can't do it by myself, Cori. I need you."

"Aw, sweetheart, I wish I could be there for you." She pulled her close again. "How did you get away? What did your mother say?"

Katie sobbed harder, so Corrine stopped asking questions and just held her while she cried.

When Katie had calmed a bit, Corrine grabbed her suitcase and led her into her living room. They sat on the couch, and Corrine put her arm around Katie. "Now then, that's enough with the tears."

Katie started crying again. "You don't understand. I miss you and they took Spirit and Mama's going to die."

Corrine set Katie an arm's length away. "I miss you, too, Katie. More than you could know. But what's this about Spirit, and what on earth do you mean Della's going to die?"

In between sobs, Katie said, "They left in the middle of the night and they took Spirit."

"Who did, sweetheart?"

"The Flanagans."

"Good riddance, I say. Though I'm sorry to hear about Spirit. Now about your mother?"

"Oh, Cori!" She sobbed uncontrollably again.

Fear gripped Corrine, and she pulled Katie close again, as much for her own comfort as Katie's.

When Katie could speak, she pulled away from Corrine and held her hands. "Mama has consumption. Dr. Logan says she's going to die."

"Then what are you doing here? Please don't misunderstand. I'm very happy to see you. But shouldn't you be tending to Della?"

"Dr. Logan sent a nurse to care for her. They don't even want me near her. It's very contagious, and they're worried I'll catch my death from it."

"I couldn't stand to lose you like that," Corrine said.

"I didn't know what else to do," Katie said. "I can't do it alone. I need you with me, so I came to see you."

"You know I can't go back there with you."

"I want you to, though."

"I'd love to, but it wouldn't be right. Does anyone know you're here?"

"No. Maybe Jacques because he took me to the dock, but Mama doesn't know, if that's what you're asking."

Corrine tried to absorb everything, but it was all coming at her so quickly. She looked at Katie with her eyes swollen and face red. "You must be exhausted. Let's get you some rest and then we'll talk about you going home."

"I don't want to go home! Don't you see? I belong with you. And I can't be with Mama anyway. I should stay here."

"Either way, we'll talk about it when you wake up."

She kept her arms around Katie and walked her to the bedroom. Katie snuggled into Corrine's arms and fell right to sleep while Corrine lay there, mind racing.

Chapter Sixteen

It was early afternoon when they finally stirred. Corrine had dozed off and on as she held Katie. Katie slept hard, burrowing deep into Corrine. Corrine smiled as she watched Katie look around, disoriented, and was greeted with a brilliant smile once she remembered where she was.

"I'm sorry," Katie said. "I came all this way to see you and promptly fell asleep. How rude."

"Not rude at all. You were tired." Corrine fingered the top of Katie's breasts. "Besides, I'm sure you'll make it up to me."

Fire seared Katie's body at Corrine's touch. She pulled her bodice down and allowed her breasts to fall free for Corrine's taking.

"Are you in a hurry then?" Corrine laughed.

"I need you, Cori. It's been far too long." She took a breast in her hands and offered it to Corrine, who sucked as if she depended on its nourishment to survive. She licked the erect nipple and then the whole breast. From the base to the tip of the nipple, she licked, sending chills coursing through Katie.

"Help me out of this dress," Katie said.

Corrine happily obliged, and Katic felt her clit swell as Corrine climbed between her legs. She moved her shoulders under Katie's knees, and Katie could feel her hot breath on her. She gasped when Corrine moved her tongue along her.

"Oh, yes. I've missed you so."

"And I you." Corrine rested her cheek in Katie's wetness and sucked her inner thigh. She was leaving a mark, branding Katie as hers.

Katie craned her neck to watch Corrine. "That feels divine. Please don't stop."

Corrine moved higher on her thigh as she sucked her again. Her mouth so close to Katie had Katie's twat twitching. "Suck my cunt like that," Katie pleaded.

Corrine pulled hard on Katie's lips with her mouth, sucking them deep. She ran her tongue along them, and Katie was lost in the sensations. She wanted more, needed more. She reached down and lightly rubbed her clit while Corrine buried her tongue inside her.

Corrine playfully moved Katie's hand away. "That's mine." She took it in her mouth. She held the swollen clit between her teeth and flicked the tip of it with her tongue.

"Oh, yes, Cori. Oh, dear Lord, how you make me feel."

She was so excited, she was confused. She wanted Cori to keep her mouth on her. She wanted to roll Cori over and fuck her. She wanted Cori in her. Her whole body was alive with desire, and she forced herself to lay back and experience the pleasure.

She felt Cori spread her opening and run a finger along it.

"Please. Fill me. I need to feel you inside me."

She watched as Corrine opened a dresser drawer and withdrew a long cylindrical leather object. It was two inches in diameter and eight inches long. "What's that?"

"It's called a dildo." Corrine used the toy to slap Katie's inner thighs. Katie responded by opening them wider. She felt the tip of the dildo on her cunt, and her throbbing renewed as she watched Corrine watch the object slide inside her.

She felt the tip of it pressing against her deeper than anyone had ever been. She arched her hips to take more and rotated them to feel it against every inch inside.

"You like that?" Corrine pressed it as deep as she dared.

"It feels heavenly."

Corrine lay next to her and bit her nipple as she pulled the dildo out of Katie.

Katie whimpered at her sudden emptiness and was rewarded when Corrine drove the tool back in.

"I love it when you fuck me hard."

"I love to fuck you hard." She withdrew the toy again before slipping it deep.

Katie was a jumble of nerves, and Corrine continued to bite her tit and fuck her with the toy. Her head spun at the onslaught of sensations. She reached down again and felt her engorged clit.

Corrine let loose of the nipple and moved to watch Katie diddle herself. The sight made her cunt throb, and she fought to keep her focus on Katie. She watched as Katie's skilled fingers rubbed circles on her clit as her cunt swallowed more and more of the dildo.

She moved the dildo in and out as fast as she could, matching Katie's bucking hips. She heard Katie scream and let go of the toy, watching her cunt suck it in and release it with each orgasmic contraction.

When Katie could finally speak, she asked, "May I keep that inside me forever, please?"

Corrine laughed. "Wouldn't that be nice?"

She withdrew the dildo and held it pointing up on her mound where her legs met. "Climb up on it."

Katie stared in disbelief.

"Come on. It'll feel even better this way."

She helped Katie straddle the toy and watched as she lowered her cunt onto it.

"Oh, my God. This fills me even more!" She leaned forward and placed her hands on either side of Corrine's head as she allowed part of the dildo to slide out. She lowered her hips and filled herself again.

She kissed Corrine hard, frantically devouring her mouth as her cunt devoured the tool.

"Sit up and bounce on it," Corrine instructed, and Katie did as she was told. She bobbed up and down, impaling herself over and over. She moved her hands to her breasts and squeezed and pinched her nipples as she rode, finally burying the tool inside her as she climaxed again and again.

She climbed off the toy and lay on her side next to Corrine. She kissed Corrine again and took the dildo from her. She deftly slid it inside Corrine and drilled her, loving the feel of it entering so easily.

Corrine opened her legs wider, and Katie climbed between them, sucking on her turgid clit while she fucked her with the tool.

"Oh, Katie, yes. That's the way." Corrine moaned, her body burning with the passion Katie evoked. She closed her eyes and felt. Thought left her. She could do nothing but experience the marvel of Katie's lovemaking. At last, she shuddered, convulsing on the dildo, giving herself over to the orgasm crashing through her.

Famished, they finally got out of bed and made themselves a snack. When their energy was restored, they fell back into bed where Corrine moved once again between Katie's legs. She slipped her tongue deep inside her, then dragged it over her slick clit.

"You taste so wonderful," she murmured. "I want always to feast on you like this."

"Please do." Katie rested her hand on Corrine's head and held her in place while she moved her hips against her.

Her mouth still on Katie's clit, Corrine moved four fingers inside her and hammered away at her dripping cunt. She stroked them back and forth along her soft walls and was rewarded when they began to spasm, finally contorting painfully around her.

Not to be outdone, Katie sucked and bit Corrine's hard nipples while she fucked her with three fingers. Corrine's cunt was wet and ready for her, and she easily slid another finger inside.

"Your hand, baby," Corrine said. "I want your whole hand inside me."

Katie was between Corrine's legs then, gaze focused on Corrine as she took her whole hand inside her. "It's so tight in there. It's hard to move."

"Don't hold back. You can move, and I want you to. Fuck me hard, Katie. Make a fist and punch my cunt."

Katie did as she was instructed and almost came at the sensation of Corrine's walls pressing her knuckles.

"Twist it around now. Oh, yes, that's it." Corrine met each of Katie's thrusts.

Katie lowered her mouth to Corrine's clit, and that was all it took for Corrine to explode in an orgasm more intense than any she'd experienced.

"Oh, God. That was amazing." She fought to catch her breath.

Katie withdrew her hand and lay against Corrine, resting her head on her chest.

"I love you, Katie," Corrine said.

"And I you," Katie whispered before they fell asleep.

Katie and Corrine awoke the next morning and made love slowly and gently, both ginger from the previous day's activities. Tongues pleased rather than dildos. Mouths worked instead of fists. They took each other repeatedly until they were completely spent.

"We should get dressed so I can take you out to eat," Corrine said.

Katie ran her hand over Corrine's folds. "I have all I want to eat right here."

Corrine laughed. "I love how much you enjoy making love."

"I can't imagine anything I'd rather do."

"I'm in complete agreement with that."

Corrine propped herself up on an elbow and grew serious. "You know your mother is worried sick about you. I fear I must insist you get back to her."

"But what about us? What about this?"

"I've decided to accompany you back home."

"You have? Oh, Cori, that's wonderful. Thank you so much."

"Perhaps they limit your time with her, but you should still be there. She needs you."

"And I need you."

"And I shall be there for you."

"What will you say to my mother?"

"I'll think of something. But I can't stand to be away from you again. We'll get through this together."

A tear spilled out of Katie's eye. "I'm so happy I'll not have to leave you."

Corrine kissed away the tear. "I hope you shall never have to again. Now let's get dressed and eat something and head to the boat. One should be leaving within the hour."

The ride on the boat was tense for Corrine. She knew she was doing the right thing, going home with Katie, but she dreaded confronting Della. Especially since she was on her deathbed. But the idea of being away from Katie any longer made her heart hurt and she knew she had to stand up to Della and fight for the right to spend eternity with Katie.

❖

It was early morning again when Katie let them into the house. They went directly to her room and washed up, then climbed into bed, exhausted.

Katie awoke later and immediately went to her mother's room.

"Where have you been, young lady? I've been worried sick about you."

Sarah joined in. "It doesn't do your mother well at all to be as upset as she's been. You should have said something before disappearing like you did."

"You told me to do something for me."

"I didn't mean run off and not say anything."

"Where were you?" her mother asked again.

"I just needed some time alone."

"I'm not long for this world," her mother said. "I didn't want to pass on not knowing where my only child was."

"She was with me."

All heads turned as Corrine entered the room.

"What are you doing here?" her mother asked.

"I came to see you. I love you, Della and couldn't stand the idea of not saying good-bye."

"We've said our good-byes."

"I also came because I love Katie and couldn't bear the thought of her going through this alone."

"Sarah, if you'll excuse us, please," her mother said.

With Sarah out of the room, she continued. "I won't be around much longer now. Why must you show up and ruin what little time I have left?"

"Della, we've been friends for as long as either of us can remember. I can't imagine not being here for you at the end, regardless of our differences."

"Our differences? You seduced my daughter. That's more than a mere difference."

"And I've explained it's more than a simple seduction. When Katie felt overwhelmed and out of control, to whom did she turn? Me. And who's here by her side in bad times as well as the good?"

Me. I love your daughter. I'm good for her. I'll take good care of her. You must believe that."

Katie moved to where Corrine stood and wrapped her arms around her. "Mama, I need Cori in my life. It's far too empty without her."

Corrine wrapped an arm around Katie and held her close. "Look at us. Look how happy we make each other. See that we belong together. We love each other and need each other. I'm not some horrible monster toying with your daughter's emotions. I love her. I want always to make her as happy as she possibly can be. Please. Life's too short to let a chance at true love pass you by. You had that with Theodore. Please let Katie have that with me."

"You really do love her, don't you?"

"I do. More than anything."

"And Katie?"

"I love her so very much, Mama. Please give us your blessing."

Corrine held her breath as Della looked from her to Katie and back. She leaned her head back against her pillow with a heavy sigh.

"Very well then. If you promise always to take care of her, Cori."

"Always. She'll never want for anything if I can help it."

"Then you have my blessing. And know I'll be watching you from wherever I end up."

"Thank you, Della."

Katie bent to hug her mother.

Della closed her eyes and repeated quietly, "Promise me you'll take care of her."

"Until I take my last breath. You've always been my dearest friend, Della. I'll always love you. And I'll always love your daughter. Thank you for trusting her to me."

Della smiled as she drifted off.

Corrine gathered Sarah, who examined Della. "She's near the end now," she said. "She could go any minute."

Katie bit her lower lip and tried to fight the ever-present tears. Not trusting her voice, she simply nodded. She looked at Corrine. "Will you find Jacques? He should collect Father O'Malley."

Corrine did as she was asked, and with Jacques dispatched to town yet again, she went back to Della's room to sit vigil with Katie.

Katie took her hand as soon as she sat down and turned to face Corrine.

"You meant what you said, didn't you? You'll always take care of me?"

"I will. For as long as you'll allow."

"I'll allow forever." Katie squeezed her hand as she turned back to her mother.

Katie and Corrine sat quietly when the priest arrived. Jacques had collected Dr. Logan as well, and he hovered in the corner with Sarah while the priest performed his ritual and blessed her mother. They watched him anoint her with holy oil as he prayed quietly, delivering the extreme unction. He tried unsuccessfully to wake her to hear her confession and deliver the Eucharist. Instead, he absolved her of her sins and made a final sign of the cross over her. Katie thanked him for coming, and he let himself out, leaving them to simply wait.

There was no sound in the room save for the labored wheezing of her mother's breath. It was rhythmic and peaceful. And then it stopped.

The room was silent as Dr. Logan checked her and pronounced her gone.

Katie's wail pierced the silence. Corrine took her in her arms and tried to soothe her, but nothing would calm her. Both her parents had left her in a matter of years, and she felt like a small child, orphaned and lost.

Corrine took Katie to her room so the doctor could see to her mother's body. She lay in bed with her, holding her and letting her cry.

CHAPTER SEVENTEEN

Corrine saw to all the details concerning Della's death. She stood by Katie as she accepted condolences and food from friends and neighbors who stopped by to pay their respects.

Three days after her death, Della's body was taken to the church where a funeral Mass was held, followed by the procession to the cemetery. With Della interred, Corrine took Katie home and put her to bed, where she stayed for the next few weeks.

Emotionally drained and overly distraught, Katie couldn't summon the energy to deal with everyday life. She completely withdrew from everyone save Corrine, who took food and drink to her and forced her to partake of it. Katie would comply and visit briefly with Corrine, thanking her for everything, then slide back under the covers.

Corrine's heart ached for her, but she knew only time would heal the deep wound inside her. Her body also ached for Katie. She finally gave up sleeping with her, as her desires were overwhelming. She retreated to her own room at night and waited patiently for Katie to come back to life.

Corrine barely convinced Katie to receive the solicitor when he came to discuss Della's will. Katie insisted he come to her room, as the effort to dress and go downstairs was too great. She cried softly as the attorney explained that Della had left everything to her with no contingencies.

Corrine stared wistfully at Katie, wondering if she'd ever have the strength to take over the plantation. In the meantime, Corrine tended to the running of the house, including acquiring a new woman to run the kitchen and promoting Jacques to running the stables.

❖

One morning, Corrine was in the breakfast nook enjoying a cup of coffee in the warm sun when Katie walked in.

Corrine stood. "Katie! What are you doing up?"

"It's time."

"I'm happy to see you up and about. Please sit down. I'll have Maddy get you something to eat."

When she returned from the kitchen, she asked, "How are you feeling?"

"Like I miss my mama, but it won't do to hide from the world forever. Thank you so much for caring for me. And for being patient with me."

"I knew you'd come around eventually. Although I admit I expected it to happen sooner."

"I'm sorry."

"No, no. Everyone deals with these things at her own pace. You've suffered some terrific losses of late."

"I'm so thankful I didn't lose you, as well."

"I'd never allow that to happen. What made you decide this was the day to rejoin the land of the living?"

"I feel like I have some energy. I haven't for a long while."

"Well, don't overdo it. You've been in bed for several weeks now."

"I've been in bed alone for all that time," she said.

"I'm aware."

"Maybe some overdoing is just what I need." She smiled mischievously.

Corrine smiled as her crotch twitched, but before she could reply, they heard the sound of horses and saw a cloud of dust. They walked to the front of the house to investigate and saw the constable climbing down from his police wagon. Two horses were tied to the back of the wagon.

"Spirit!" Katie exclaimed and hurried down the steps and threw her arms around her horse's neck.

The constable laughed at Katie's exuberance. "I've got three people in the back of the wagon here if you'd like to take a look and let me know if they're your servants."

Corrine was at Katie's side, arm around her for support. The constable opened the back of the wagon, and there sat Paddy, Abigail, and Mollie. Katie nodded. "That's them."

"You'll be wanting them all prosecuted?"

She glared at Mollie, who glared back, cold hatred in her gaze.

"I want him to rot in prison. The others should be sent back to Ireland. They don't deserve to be in this country. While their debt to us will never be repaid, I'll feel better knowing they're back where they came from."

"As you wish," he said and closed the doors.

Corrine and Katie busied themselves untying the horses and thanked the constable before he drove off. They walked their horses back to the stables.

"Isn't it wonderful?" Katie said. "I'm so happy to have Spirit back."

"He's happy to be back, to be sure."

Corrine put the roan in its stall and watched Katie fawning over Spirit. The familiar burning in her loins was back at the sight of Katie happy again. Or at least not overly depressed. She walked up behind her and moved her hair off her neck. Pressing into her from behind, she nibbled on her neck and exposed back.

"I've missed you, Katie Prentiss."

Katie leaned back into Corrine. "I've missed you too."

Corrine placed a hand on Katie's breast. "I suspect I've missed you more."

"Only because you were conscious."

"That could be."

Corrine stepped away from Katie when they heard footsteps. Jacques walked into the stables. "Hello, Miss Katie. It's good to see you. I heard we got the horses back and had to come see."

"We did." Katie started brushing Spirit again. "And they don't look any the worse for wear."

"No, ma'am. They look pretty good."

"If you two will excuse me," Corrine said and left the two horse lovers to talk.

"I worried they may have starved, but they seem healthy, don't you think?" Katie said.

"That they do. I'll give them a thorough exam, though."

"Thank you, Jacques. Will you do so quickly? I'd like to take Spirit for a ride."

"I'll do it right now."

"And I'll be back shortly."

❖

Corrine tried to focus on some ledgers that had been delivered to her from her office, but her mind kept drifting to the feel of Katie. It had been too long, and she craved the pleasures her body provided. They were lucky they hadn't been more compromised when Jacques walked in.

She had finally settled in to work when Katie came in, dressed in her riding habit. The sight made Corrine's head swim. "Aren't you a sight for sore eyes?"

"Am I?" Katie turned away and bent to touch her toes.

"Dear God, but I love your ass."

"Do you want it?"

"I want every inch of you. I ache to have you."

"Mmm. Well, put that work aside. I've had Maddy pack us a picnic. It's far too beautiful a day to be trapped indoors. Let's go for a ride."

Corrine didn't have to be asked twice. She followed Katie to the stables and was about to throw her on the hay pile when Jacques appeared.

"Perfect timing," he said. "I just finished looking over Spirit. He's fine."

"I'm so relieved."

"Shall I saddle him for you?"

"Please. And the roan for Miss Corrine."

While Jacques busied himself with the horses, Corrine whispered in Katie's ear. "This is torture. My hands itch to run all over your body."

"Patience, sweetheart." Katie sucked on Corrine's earlobe.

"That doesn't help."

"The horses are ready. Enjoy your ride."

Corrine tried to speed up their ride, but Katie was determined to move at a leisurely pace. Corrine's clit was hard from looking at Katie and not touching. She was tempted to pull up the horses and take Katie in the middle of the fields. Instead, she exercised patience and felt her body would surely explode when they finally reached the stand of oak trees where they last had picnicked.

As soon as the horses were tied to the trees, Corrine had Katie in her arms. She bruised her lips with her kiss as her tongue moved about her mouth the way she wanted to move it inside Katie. She hastily pushed up Katie's skirt and slid her hand inside. Her rubbing was demanding, and soon Katie collapsed against her as she quickly came.

Corrine put her fingers in Katie's mouth, and every nerve ending was afire as Katie sucked her fingers clean.

Katie quickly stripped and lay on the blanket. She teased between her legs as Corrine stood over her. Corrine dropped to her knees.

"Not so fast," Katie said. "I want to watch you undress for me."

Barely able to breathe, Corrine took her shirt off quickly, so she could keep her focus on Katie's fingers and the shiny pearl that kept disappearing and reappearing under them. She stepped out of her trousers and lay atop Katie, their hardened clits pressing against each other.

She ground into Katie as she kissed her again. Katie moved her hand between them and rubbed both clits at once.

"Oh, no." Corrine groaned. "Too soon."

"Never." Katie continued to rub her fingers over herself while she pressed the back of her hand into Corrine. She rubbed frantically, and in no time, they cried out in ecstasy.

Corrine rolled off Katie and sucked a nipple while her fingers moved easily inside her. She twisted them, then separated them before pulling them out.

"You certainly enjoy teasing me, don't you?"

"I do. I love the feel of you, the sound of you. I like to experience as much of you as possible." She slid her fingers back inside and thrust them in and out while she continued to suckle Katie.

Katie tangled her fingers in Corrine's hair and watched her mouth move on her tit. White heat passed between her nipple and cunt where Corrine continued to hammer away. She moved her hips, forcing Corrine deeper.

Corrine released Katie's nipple and kissed down her belly to her upper thighs. She sucked one inner thigh and then the other, leaving love bites as she did. She finally closed her mouth on Katie's clit.

Katie threw her head back and screamed as the orgasms rolled over her. She had barely caught her breath when she felt Corrine's mouth on her again. Katie climbed on Corrine's face and put her own face between Corrine's legs. Their mouths worked in tandem on each other until neither could control herself. Together they came, nearly drowning each other in their juices.

Katie slid off Corrine's mouth and dragged her wet folds the length of her torso. She knelt between her legs and drove her fingers deep while she bent to suck her clit anew. Corrine felt the tips of Katie's fingers bumping her insides and moved her hips in rhythm with the fucking. She loved a hard fuck and wanted to prolong the feeling, but Katie had her too aroused, and she came forcefully, her twat closing tightly around Katie's fingers.

She felt Katie's hand moving inside her again, and she stopped her, pulling her up to lie in her arms. "That's enough for right now, my dear."

Katie rested her head on Corrine's chest and absently fingered a nipple.

"Look around you, Katie. All this is yours."

"Don't you mean ours? What happens next, Cori?"

"I'd like to think of it as ours."

"Will you move here and live with me? Or will you be going back to Baton Rouge?"

"That all depends on you. I've been wanting to talk with you about this, but you were never awake long enough."

"I'm awake now, and while I still want to devour your body, you have my complete attention."

"What would you like me to do?"

"I want you here with me, of course."

"I was hoping you'd say that. I've made some inquiries into selling my house and part of my business. I can still work with some clients living here."

"Cori! That's fantastic news. We shall be together forever then."

"And forever starts right now," Corrine murmured, moving between Katie's legs once more.

About the Author

MJ Williamz was raised on California's Central Coast, which she still loves, but left at the age of seventeen in an attempt to further her education. She graduated from Chico State with a degree in Business Management. It was in Chico that MJ began to pursue her love of writing.

Now living in Portland, Oregon, MJ has made writing an integral part of her life. Since 2002, she's had over two dozen short stories accepted for publication, mostly erotica with a few romances thrown in for good measure. *Forbidden Passions* is MJ's second published novel.

Books Available From Bold Strokes Books

Waiting in the Wings by Melissa Brayden. Jenna has spent her whole life training for the stage, but the one thing she didn't prepare for was Adrienne. Is she ready to sacrifice what she's worked so hard for in exchange for a shot at something much deeper? (978-1-60282-561-1)

Sex and Skateboards by Ashley Bartlett. Sex and skateboards and surfing on the California coast. What more could anyone want? Alden McKenna thinks that's all she needs, until she meets Weston Duvall. (978-1-60282-562-8)

Pirate's Fortune by Gun Brooke. Book Four in the Supreme Constellations series. Set against the backdrop of war, captured mercenary Weiss Kyakh is persuaded to work undercover with bio-android Madisyn Pimm, which foils her plans to escape, but kindles unexpected love. (978-1-60282-563-5)

Suite Nineteen by Mel Bossa. Psychic Ben Lebeau moves into Shilts Manor where he meets seductive Lennox Van Kemp and his clan of Métis—guardians of a spiritual conspiracy dating back to Christ. But are Ben's psychic abilities strong enough to save him? (978-1-60282-564-2)

Wings: Subversive Gay Angel Erotica edited by Todd Gregory. A collection of powerfully written tales of passion and desire centered on the aching beauty of angels. (978-1-60282-565-9)

Speaking Out: LGBTQ Youth Stand Up edited by Steve Berman. Inspiring stories written for and about LGBT and Q teens of overcoming adversity (against intolerance and homophobia) and experiencing life after coming out. (978-1-60282-566-6)

Forbidden Passions by MJ Williamz. Passion burns hotter when it's forbidden and the fire between Katie Prentiss and Corrine Staples in antebellum Louisiana is raging out of control. (978-1-60282-641-0)

Harmony by Karis Walsh. When Brook Stanton meets a beautiful musician who threatens the security of her conventional, predetermined future, will she take a chance on finding the harmony only love creates? (978-1-60282-237-5)

nightrise by Nell Stark and Trinity Tam. In the third book in the everafter series, when Valentine Darrow loses her soul, Alexa must cross continents to find a way to save her. (978-1-60282-238-2)

Men of the Mean Streets: Gay Noir edited by Greg Herren and J.M. Redmann. Dark tales of amorality and criminality by some of the top authors of gay mysteries. (978-1-60282-240-5)

Women of the Mean Streets: Lesbian Noir edited by J.M. Redmann and Greg Herren. Murder, mayhem, sex, and danger—these are the stories of the women who dare to tackle the mean streets. (978-1-60282-241-2)

Cool Side of the Pillow by Gill McKnight. Bebe Franklin falls for funeral director Clara Dearheart, but how can she compete with the ghost of Clara's lover—and a love that transcends death and knows no rest? (978-1-60282-633-5)

Firestorm by Radclyffe. Firefighter paramedic Mallory "Ice" James isn't happy when the undisciplined Jac Russo joins her command, but lust isn't something either can control—and they soon discover ice burns as fiercely as flame. (978-1-60282-232-0)

The Best Defense by Carsen Taite. When socialite Aimee Howard hires former homicide detective Skye Keaton to find her missing niece, she vows not to mix business with pleasure, but she soon finds Skye hard to resist. (978-1-60282-233-7)

After the Fall by Robin Summers. When the plague destroys most of humanity, Taylor Stone thinks there's nothing left to live for, until she meets Kate, a woman who makes her realize love is still alive and makes her dream of a future she thought was no longer possible. (978-1-60282-234-4)

Accidents Never Happen by David-Matthew Barnes. From the moment Albert and Joey meet by chance beneath a train track on a street in Chicago, a domino effect is triggered, setting off a chain reaction of murder and tragedy. (978-1-60282-235-1)

In Plain View by Shane Allison. Best-selling gay erotica authors create the stories of sex and desire modern readers crave. (978-1-60282-236-8)

Wild by Meghan O'Brien. Shapeshifter Selene Rhodes dreads the full moon and the loss of control it brings, but when she rescues forensic pathologist Eve Thomas from a vicious attack by a masked man, she discovers she isn't the scariest monster in San Francisco. (978-1-60282-227-6)

Reluctant Hope by Erin Dutton. Cancer survivor Addison Hunt knows she can't offer any guarantees, in love or in life, and after experiencing a loss of her own, Brooke Donahue isn't willing to risk her heart. (978-1-60282-228-3)

Conquest by Ronica Black. When Mary Brunelle stumbles into the arms of Jude Jaeger, a gorgeous dominatrix at a private nightclub, she is smitten, but she soon finds out Jude is her professor, and Professor Jaeger doesn't date her students...or her conquests. (978-1-60282-229-0)

The Affair of the Porcelain Dog by Jess Faraday. What darkness stalks the London streets at night? Ira Adler, present plaything of crime lord Cain Goddard, will soon find out. (978-1-60282-230-6)

365 Days by K.E. Payne. Life sucks when you're seventeen years old and confused about your sexuality, and the girl of your dreams doesn't even know you exist. Then in walks sexy new emo girl, Hannah Harrison. Clemmie Atkins has exactly 365 days to discover herself, and she's going to have a blast doing it! (978-1-60282-540-6)

Darkness Embraced by Winter Pennington. Surrounded by harsh vampire politics and secret ambitions, Epiphany learns that an old enemy is plotting treason against the woman she once loved, and to save all she holds dear, she must embrace and form an alliance with the dark. (978-1-60282-221-4)

78 Keys by Kristin Marra. When the cosmic powers choose Devorah Rosten to be their next gladiator, she must use her unique skills to try to save her lover, herself, and even humankind. (978-1-60282-222-1)

Playing Passion's Game by Lesley Davis. Trent Williams's only passion in life is gaming—until Juliet Sullivan makes her realize that love can be a whole different game to play. (978-1-60282-223-8)